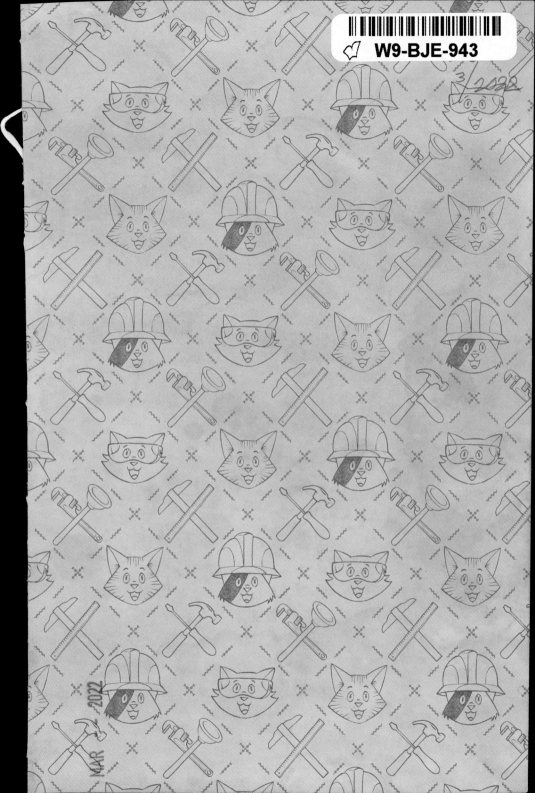

3 2022

MAR 2022

KITTEN CONSTRUCTION COMPANY

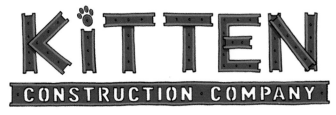

Meet the House Kittens

KITTEN

CONSTRUCTION COMPANY

Meet the House Kittens

John Patrick Green

with color by Cat Caro

:01

First Second
New York

Special thanks—
to Janelle Asselin for her fabulous feline photo skills;
to Cat, again for her amazing colors; to the entire First Second crew;
to Tory Woollcott, Kean Soo, and Reginald Barkley;
to LEGO, erector sets, Robotix, Doozers, Garfield, and Jim Davis;
to kittens everywhere; and NO THANKS to my allergies.

:01

First Second

Published by First Second
First Second is an imprint of Roaring Brook Press,
a division of Holtzbrinck Publishing Holdings Limited Partnership
120 Broadway, New York, NY 10271
firstsecondbooks.com
mackids.com

Library of Congress Cataloging-in-Publication Data is available.

Our books may be purchased in bulk for promotional, educational, or business use. Please
contact your local bookseller or the Macmillan Corporate and Premium Sales Department at
(800) 221-7945 ext. 5442 or by email at MacmillanSpecialMarkets@macmillan.com.

First edition, 2018
Revised edition, 2021

Edited by Calista Brill and Kiara Valdez
Cover design by Andrew Arnold
Interior book design by John Patrick Green
Printed in China by RR Donnelley Asia Printing Solutions Ltd.,
Dongguan City, Guangdong Province

ISBN 978-1-250-80193-7
1 3 5 7 9 10 8 6 4 2

Don't miss your next favorite book from First Second!
For the latest updates go to firstsecondnewsletter.com and sign up for our enewsletter.

For the builders

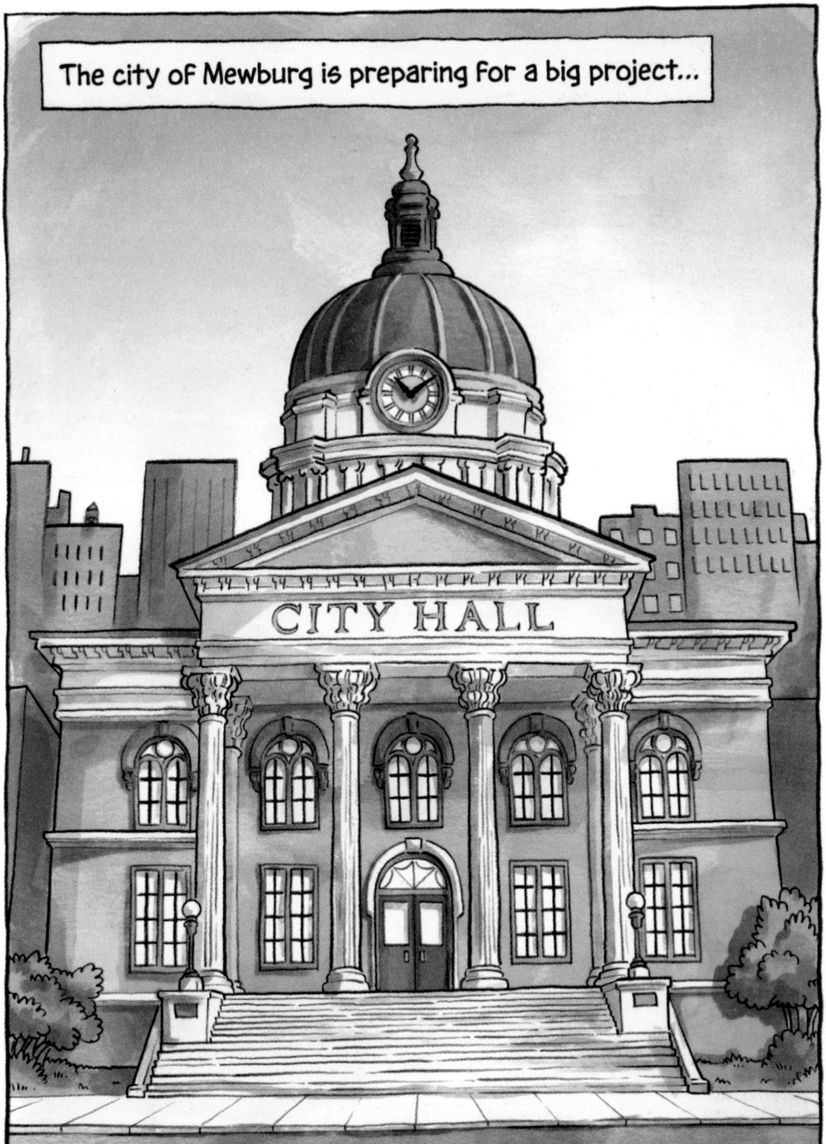
The city of Mewburg is preparing for a big project...
CITY HALL

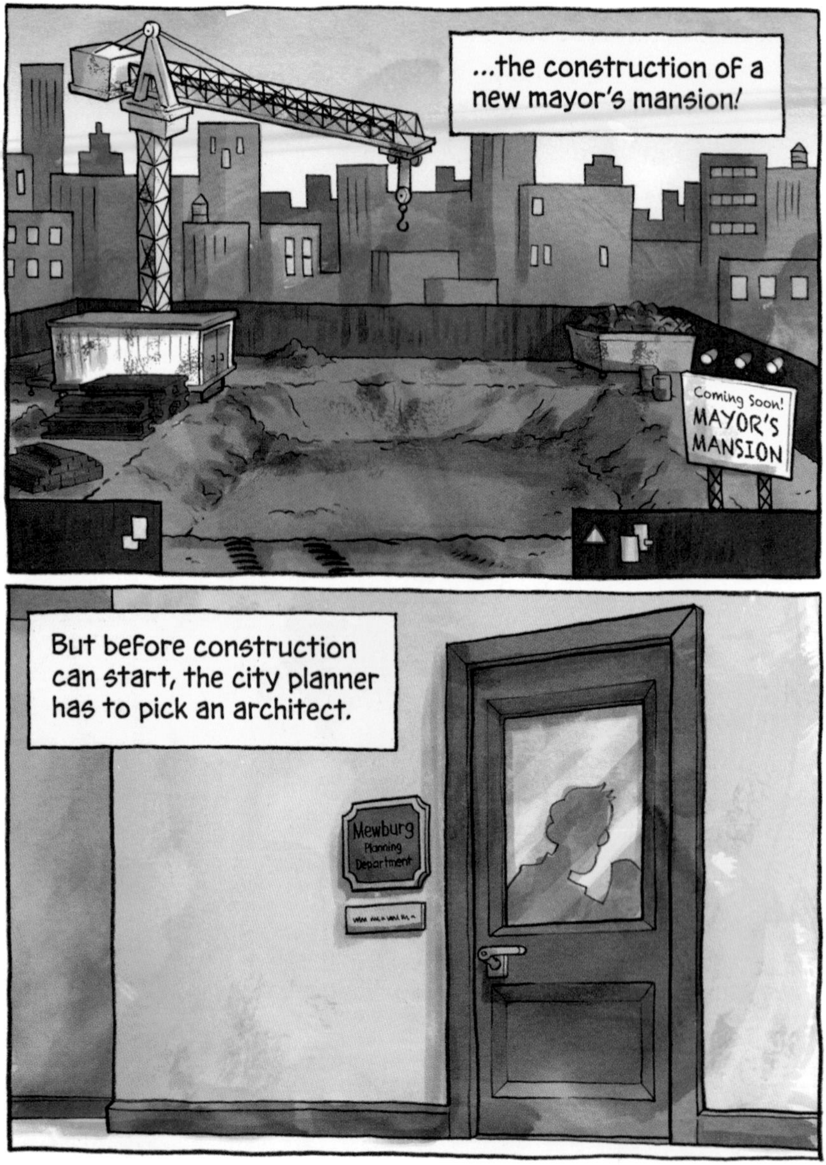
...the construction of a new mayor's mansion!
Coming Soon! MAYOR'S MANSION
But before construction can start, the city planner has to pick an architect.
Mewburg Planning Department

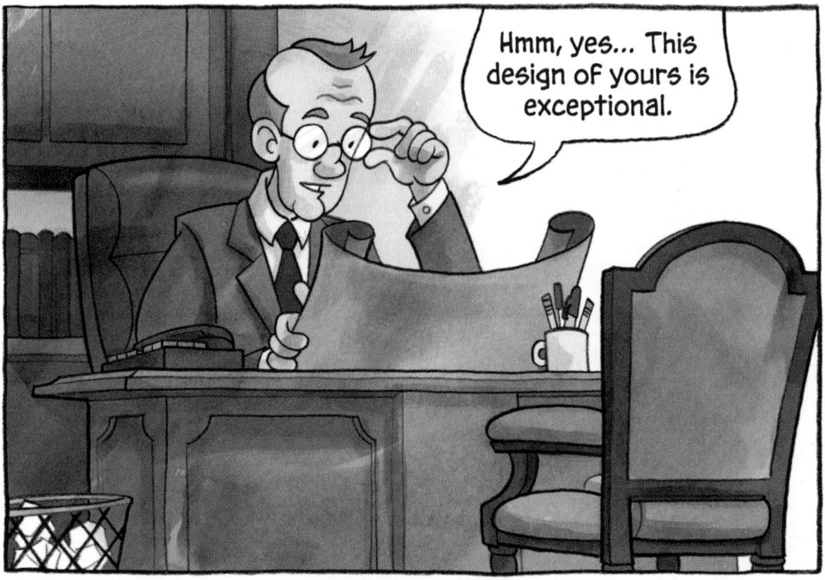
Hmm, yes... This design of yours is exceptional.

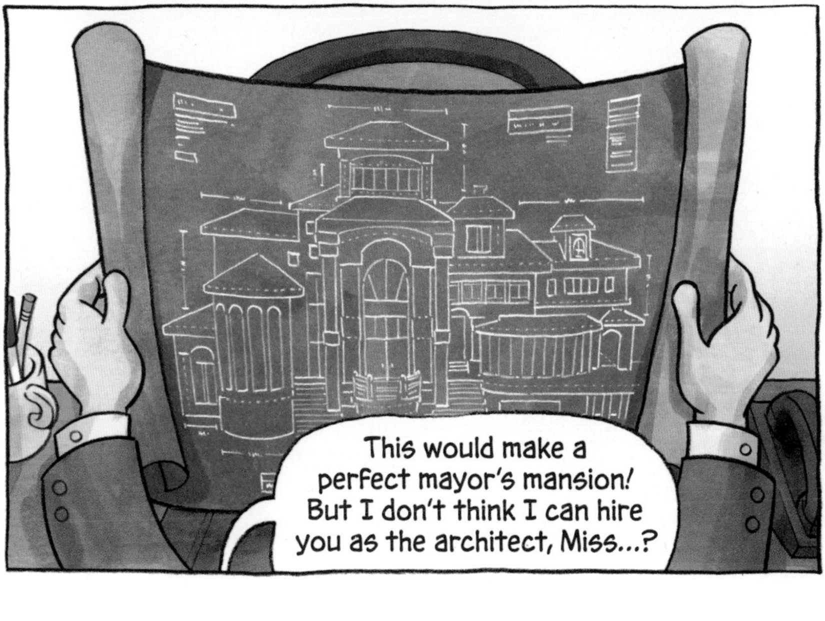
This would make a perfect mayor's mansion! But I don't think I can hire you as the architect, Miss...?

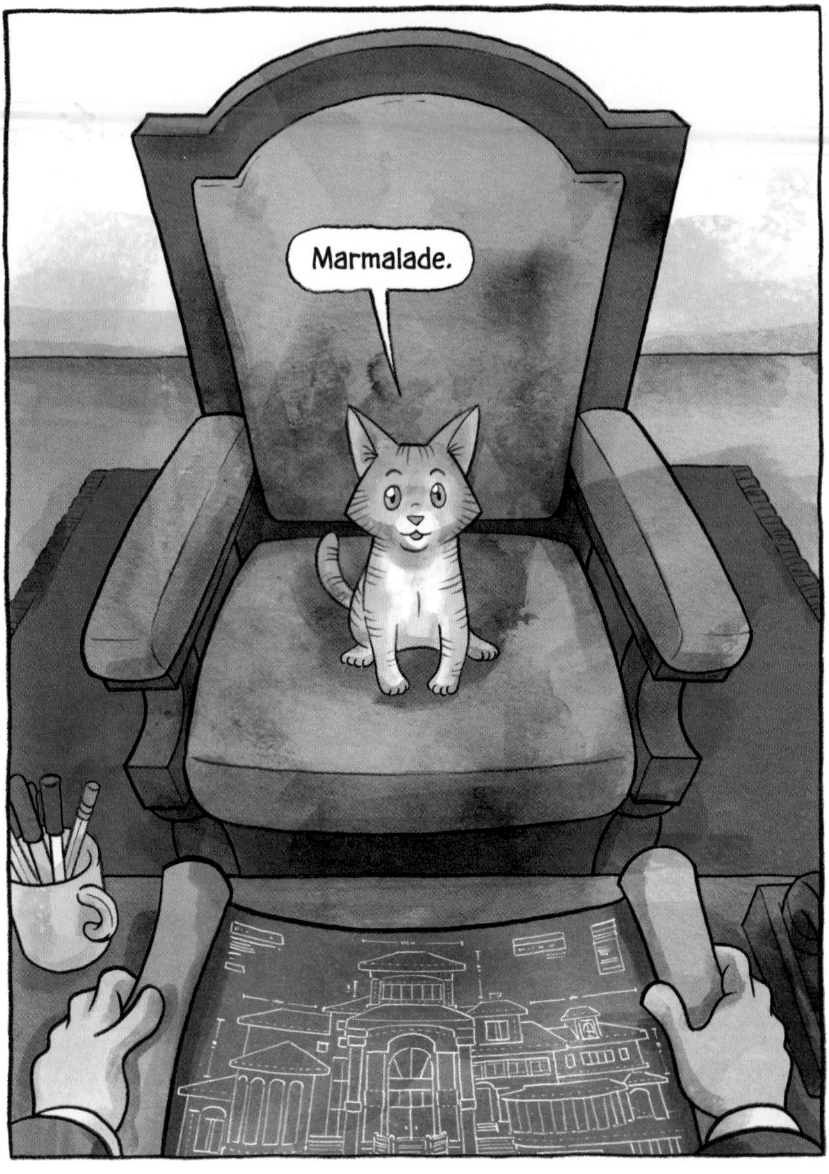
Marmalade.

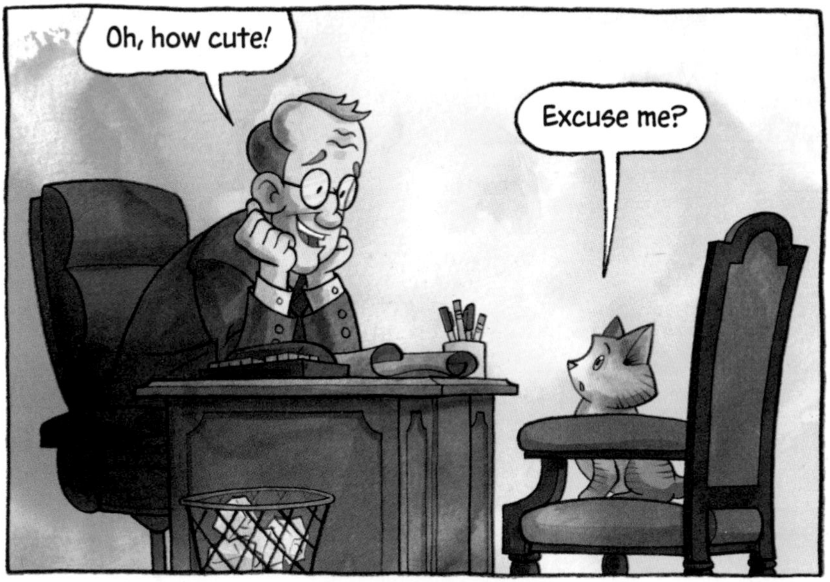
Oh, how cute!
Excuse me?

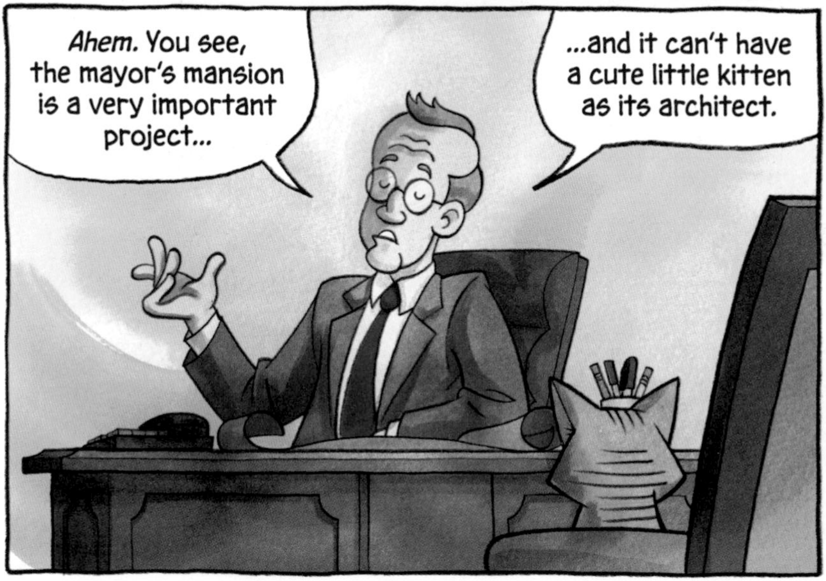
Ahem. You see, the mayor's mansion is a very important project...
...and it can't have a cute little kitten as its architect.

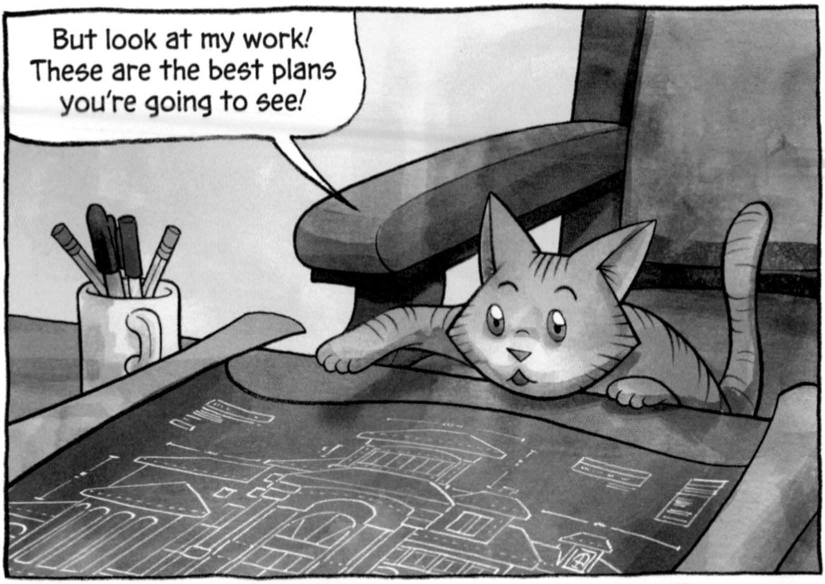
But look at my work! These are the best plans you're going to see!

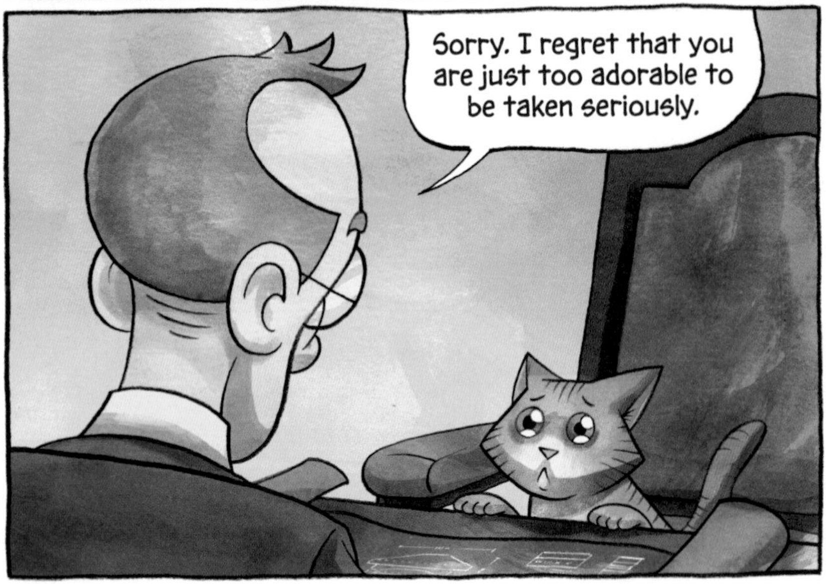
Sorry. I regret that you are just too adorable to be taken seriously.

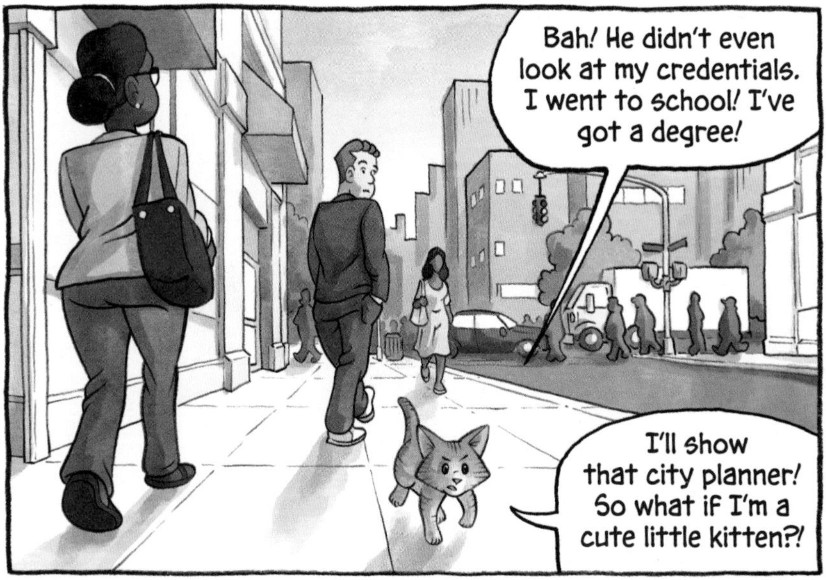
Bah! He didn't even look at my credentials. I went to school! I've got a degree!
I'll show that city planner! So what if I'm a cute little kitten?!

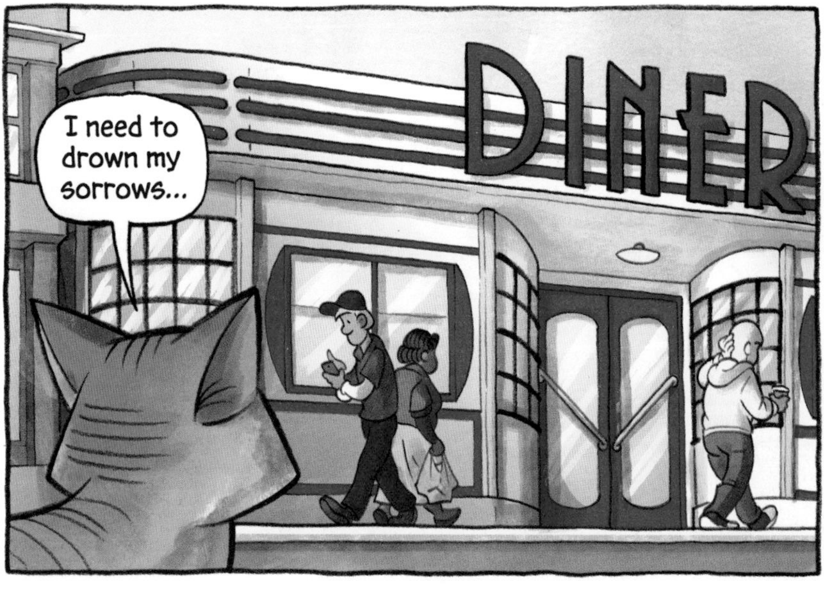
DINER
I need to drown my sorrows...

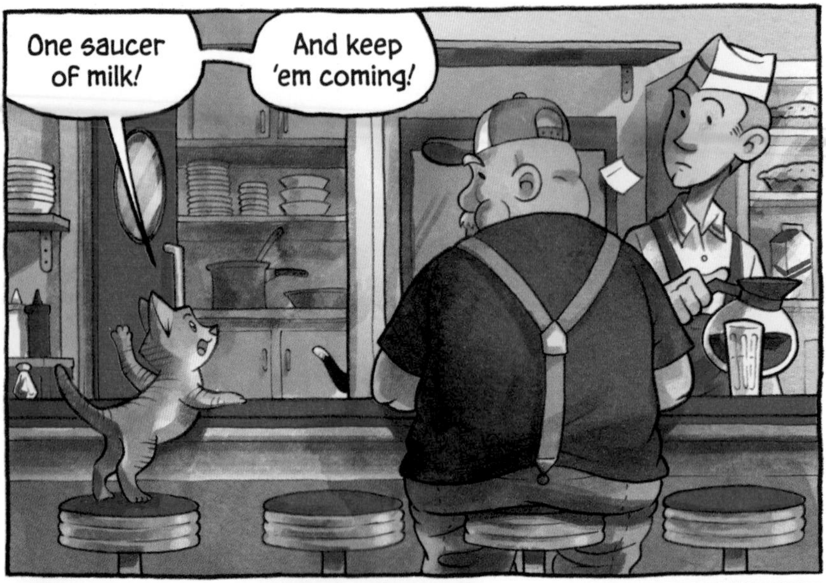
One saucer of milk!
And keep 'em coming!

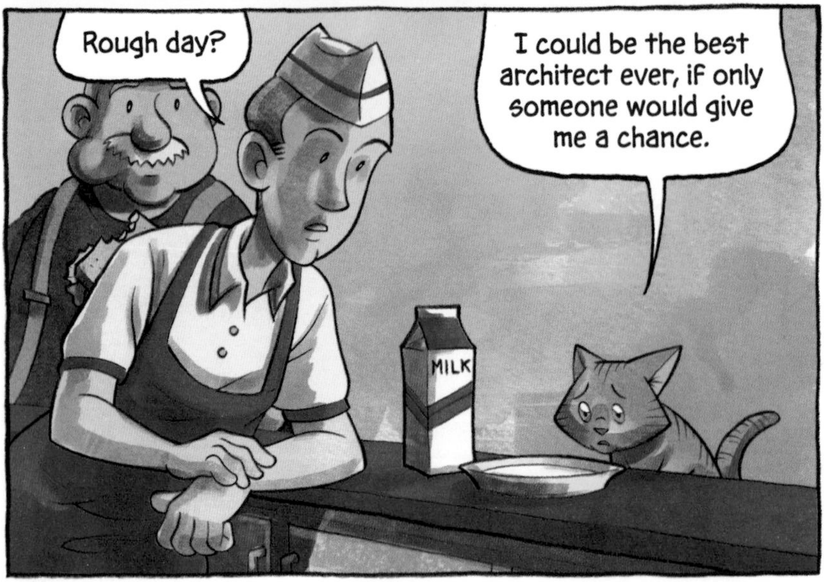
Rough day?
I could be the best architect ever, if only someone would give me a chance.
MILK

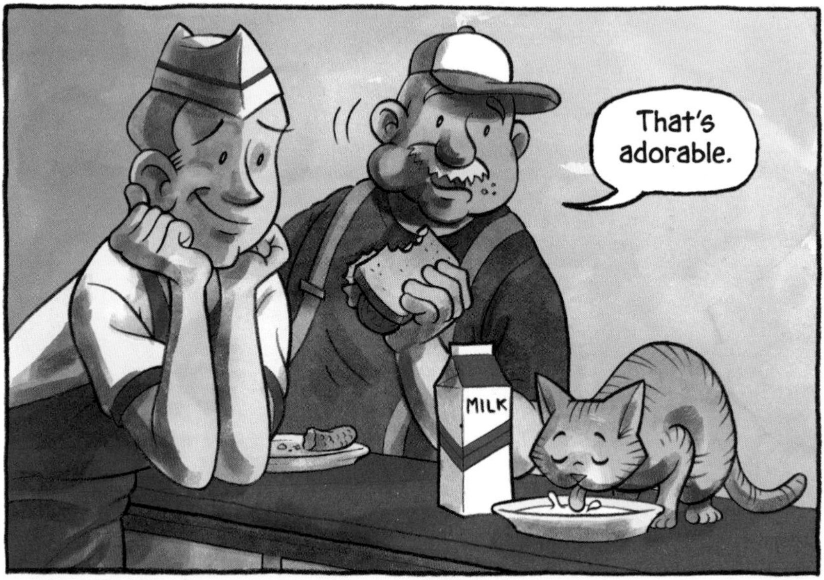
That's adorable.

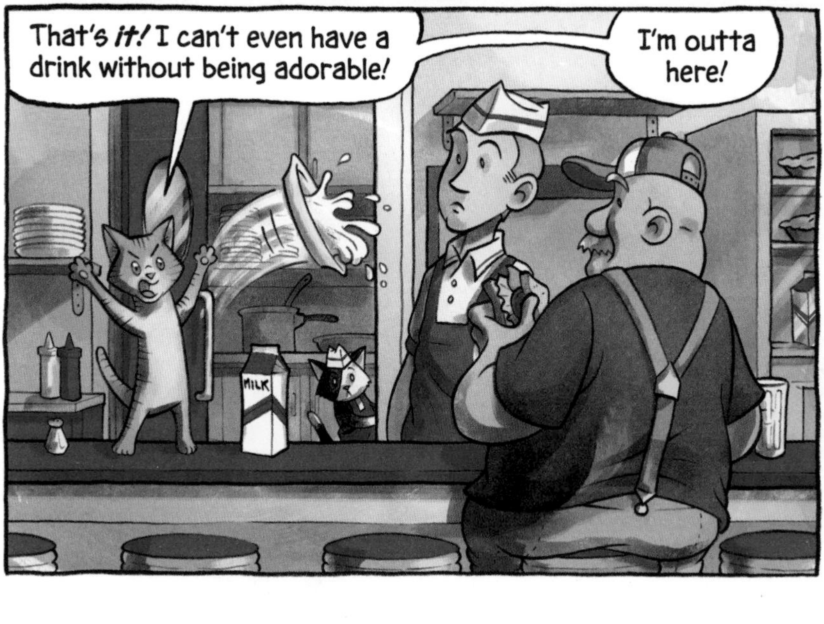
That's *it!* I can't even have a drink without being adorable!
I'm outta here!
MILK

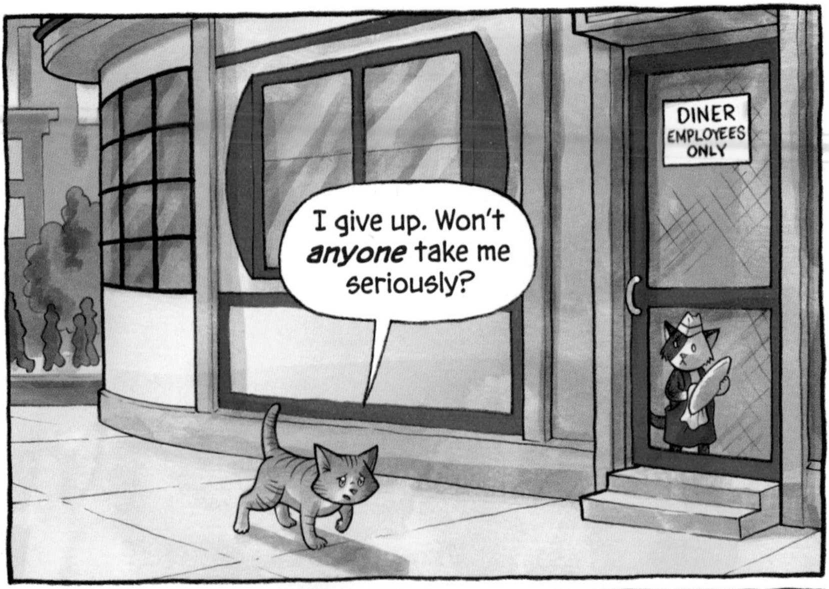
DINER
EMPLOYEES
ONLY
I give up. Won't *anyone* take me seriously?

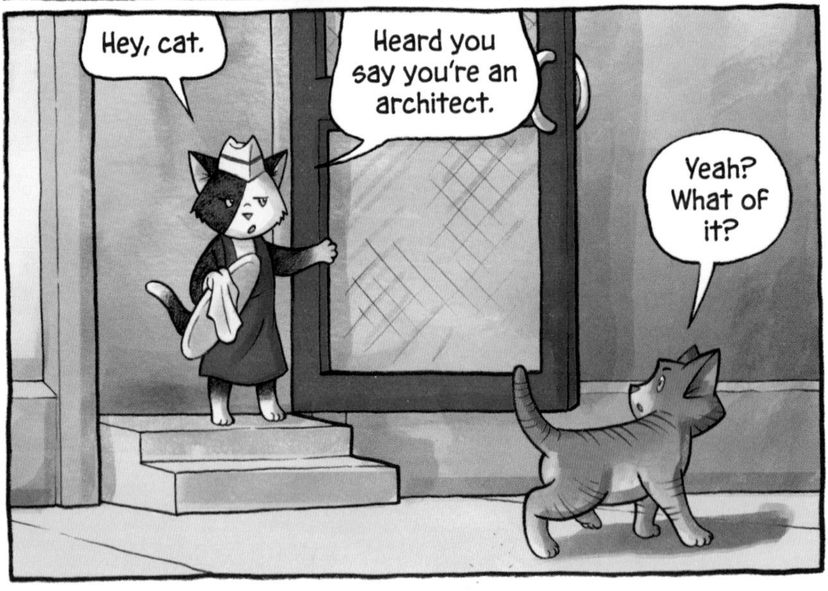
Hey, cat.
Heard you say you're an architect.
Yeah? What of it?

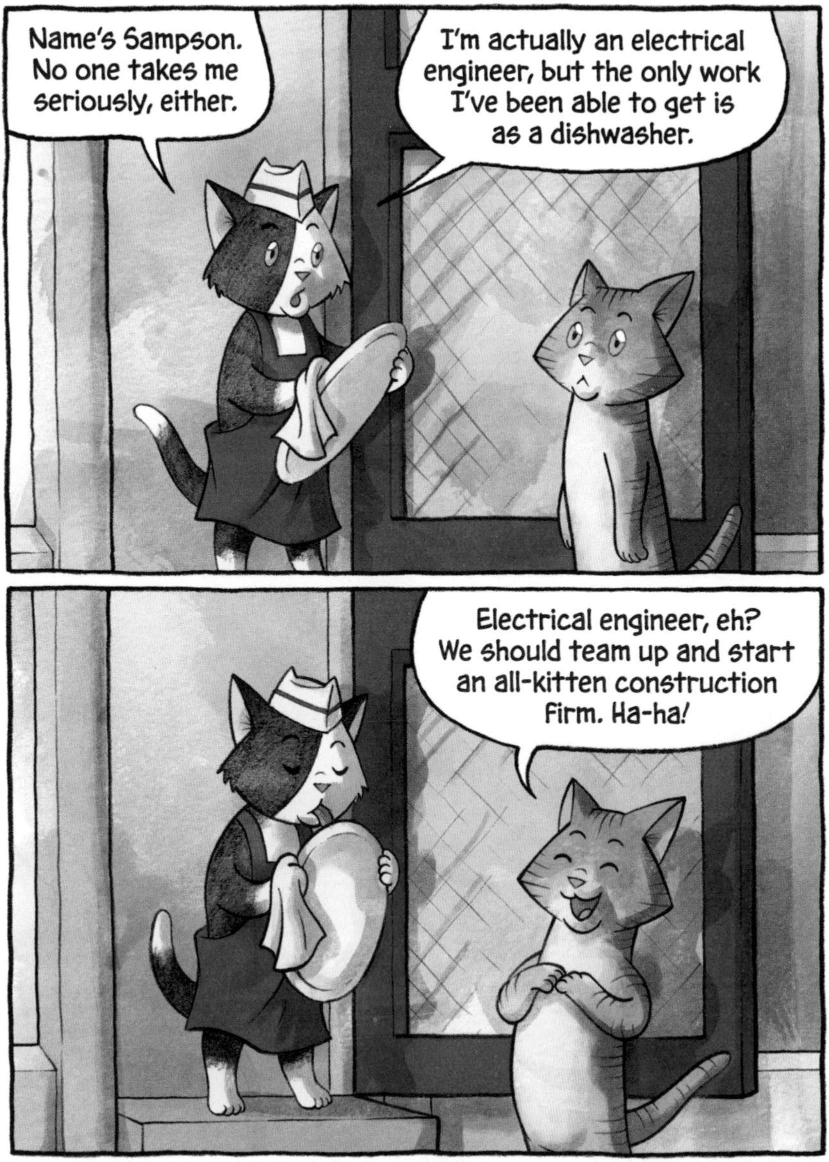
Name's Sampson. No one takes me seriously, either.
I'm actually an electrical engineer, but the only work I've been able to get is as a dishwasher.
Electrical engineer, eh? We should team up and start an all-kitten construction firm. Ha-ha!

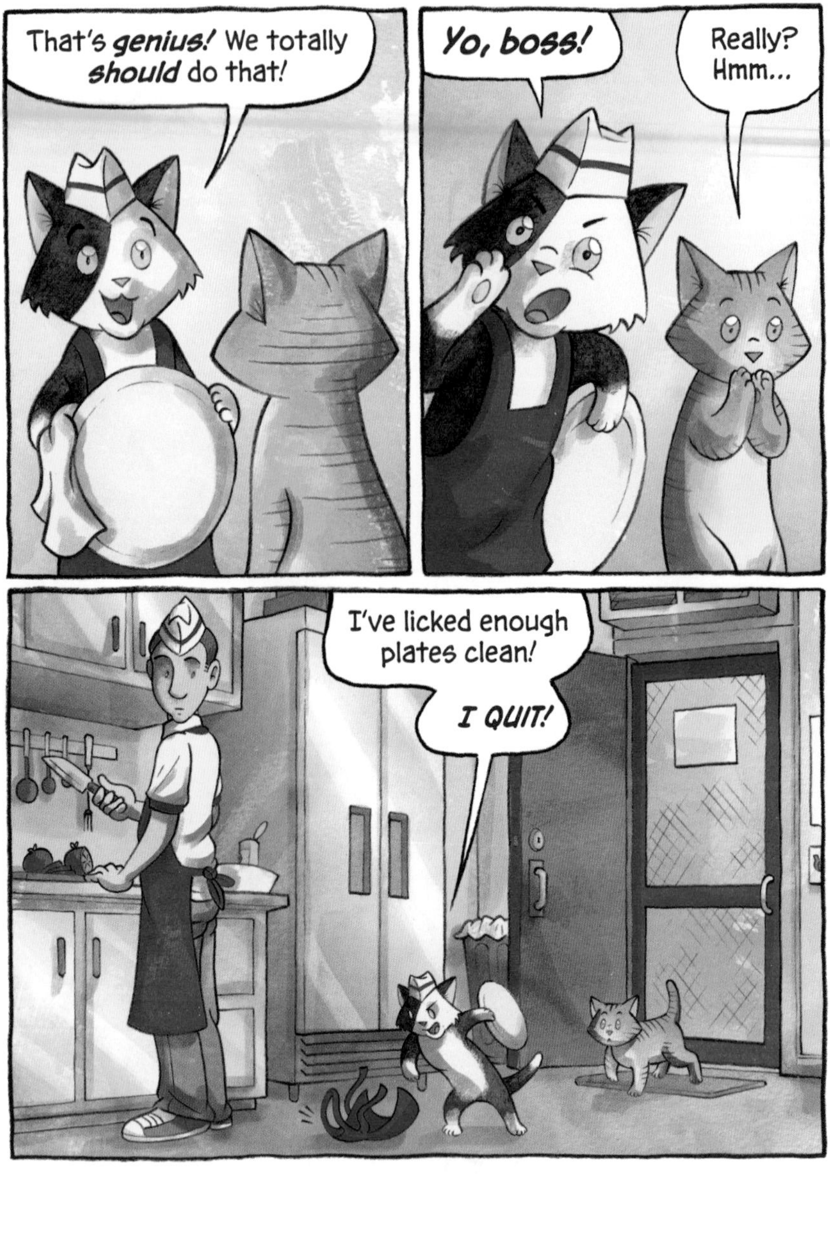
That's *genius!* We totally *should* do that!
Yo, boss!
Really? Hmm...
I've licked enough plates clean!
I QUIT!

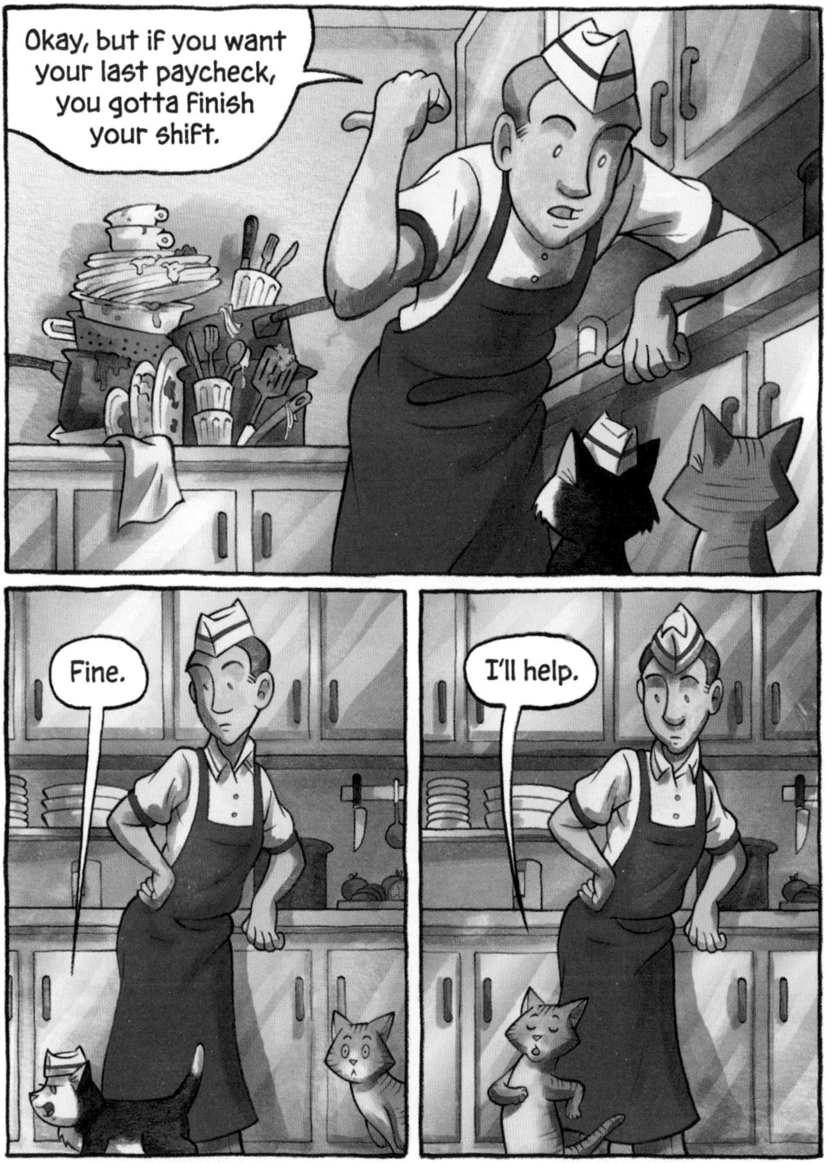
Okay, but if you want your last paycheck, you gotta finish your shift.
Fine.
I'll help.

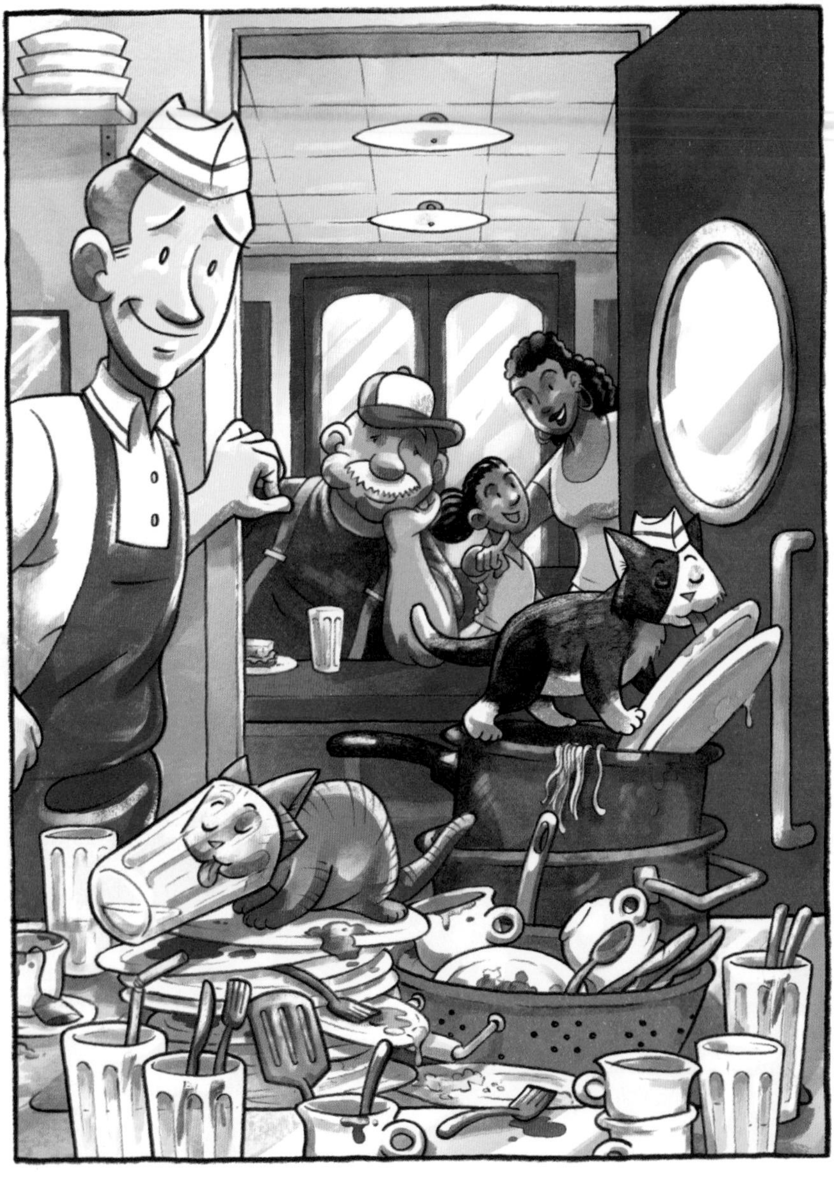

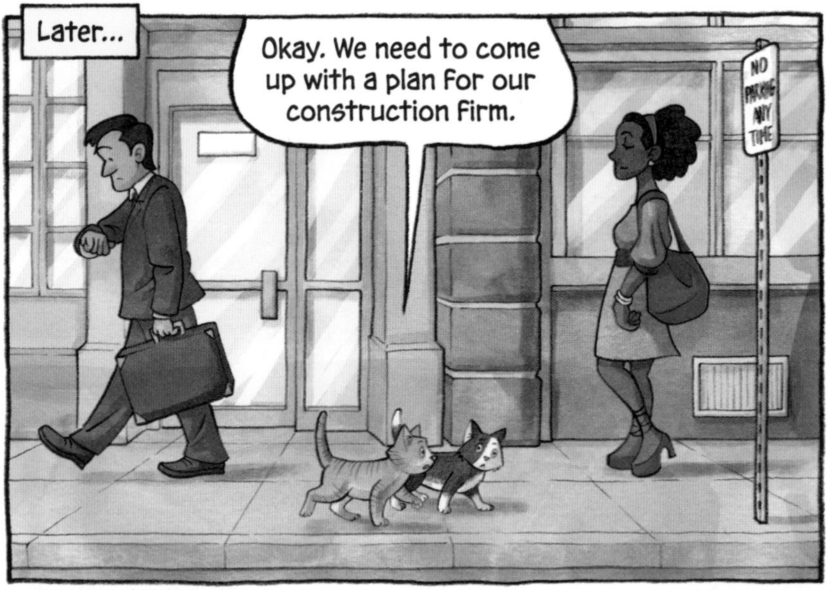
Later...
Okay. We need to come up with a plan for our construction firm.
NO PARKING ANY TIME

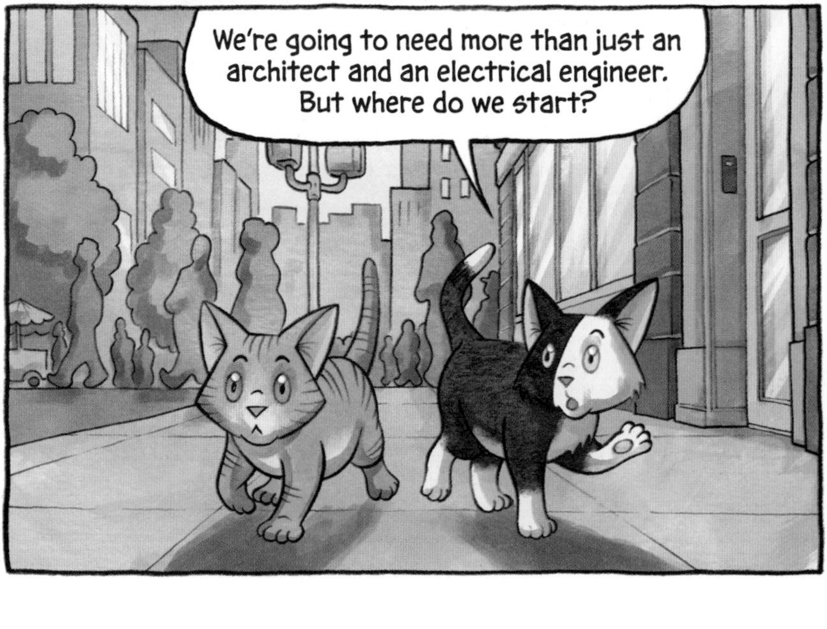
We're going to need more than just an architect and an electrical engineer. But where do we start?

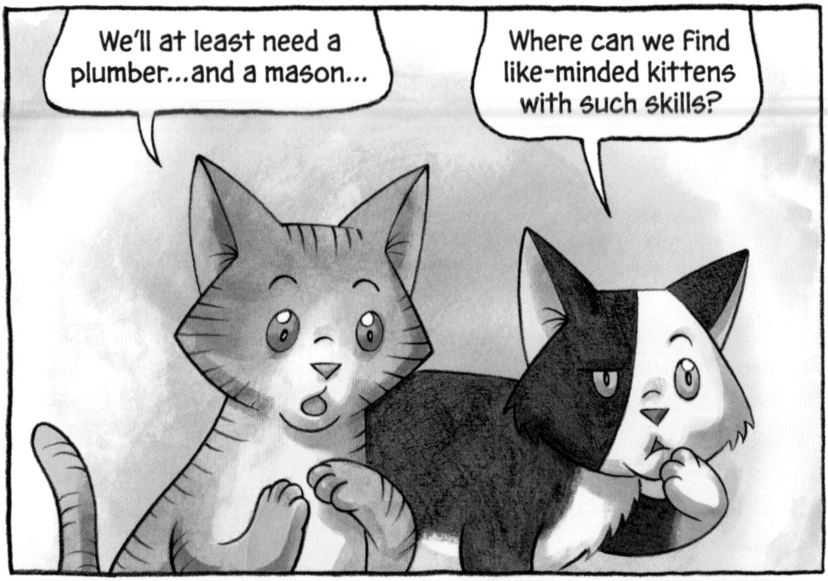
We'll at least need a plumber...and a mason...
Where can we find like-minded kittens with such skills?

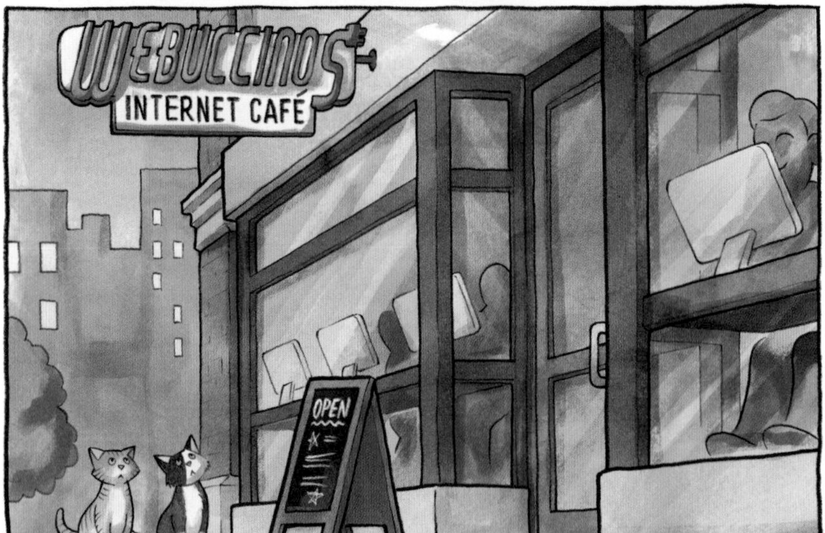
WEBUCCINOS
INTERNET CAFÉ
OPEN

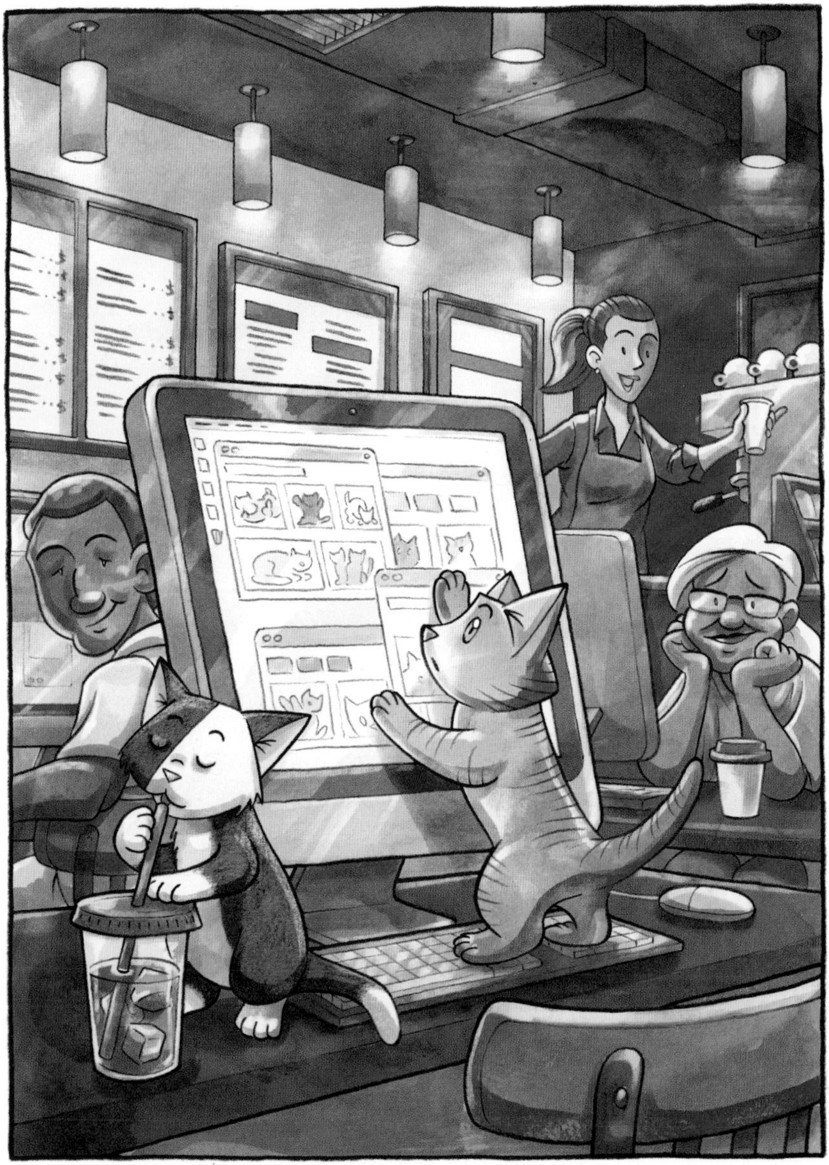

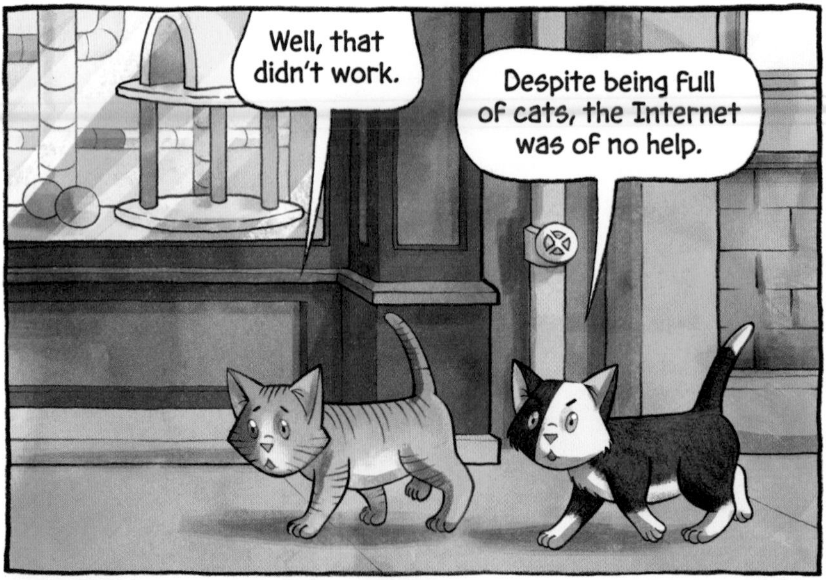
Well, that didn't work.
Despite being full of cats, the Internet was of no help.

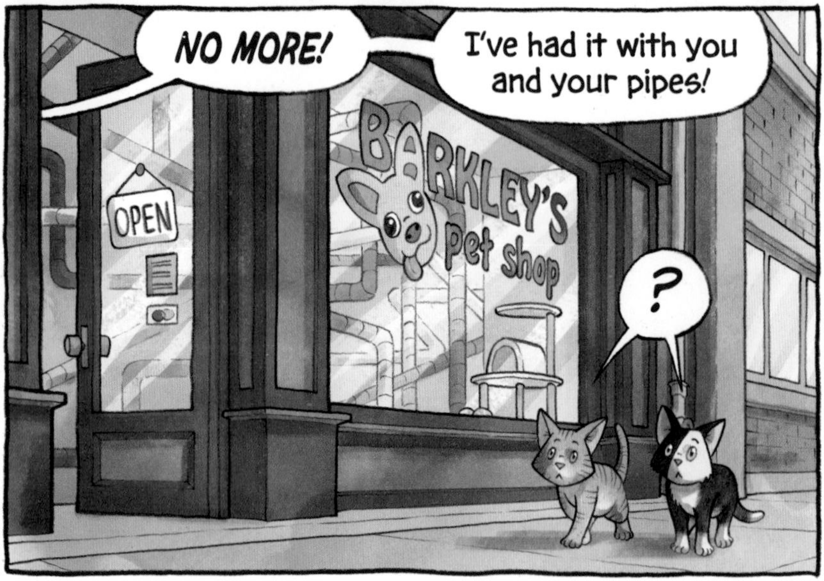
NO MORE!
I've had it with you and your pipes!
OPEN
BARKLEY'S pet shop
?

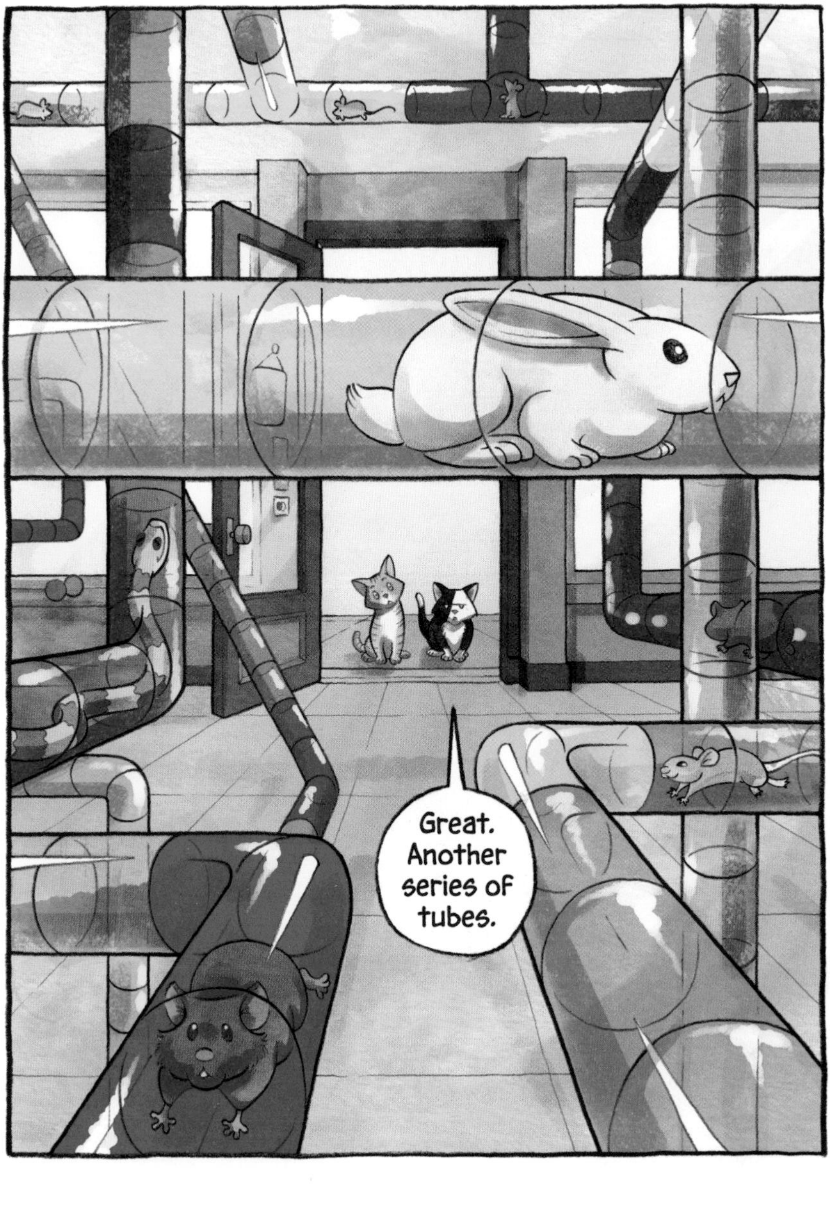
Great. Another series of tubes.

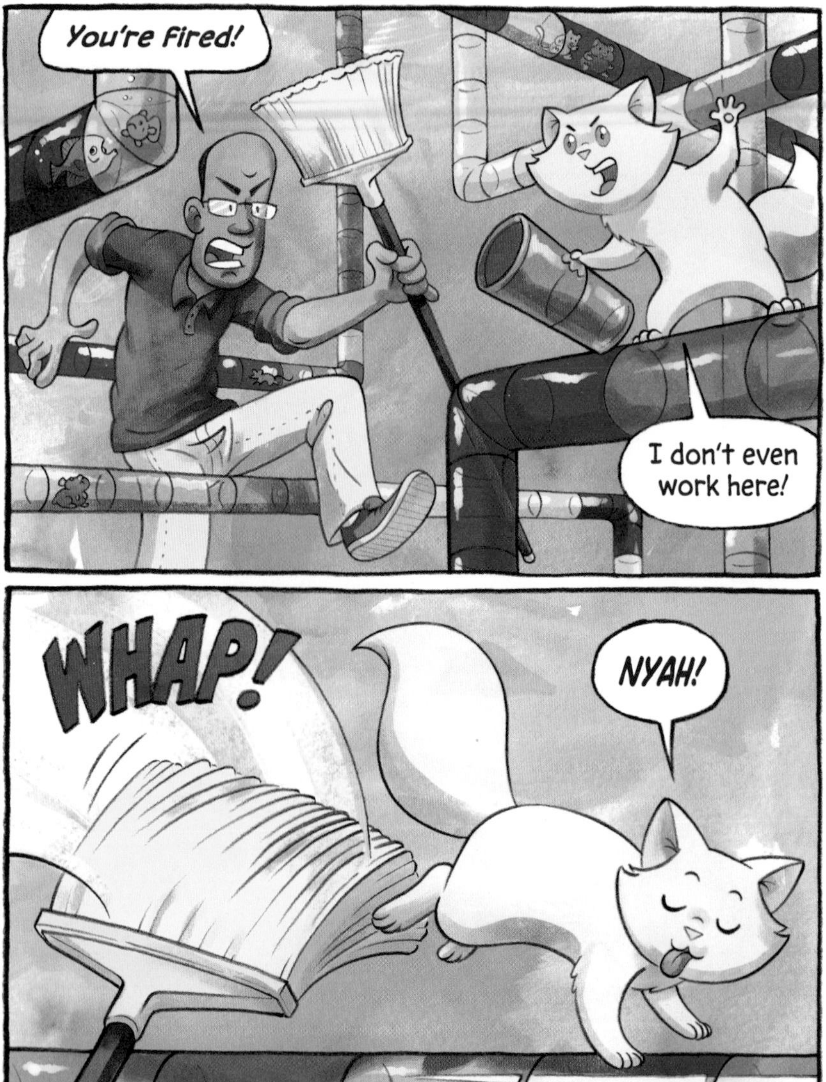
You're Fired!
I don't even work here!
WHAP!
NYAH!

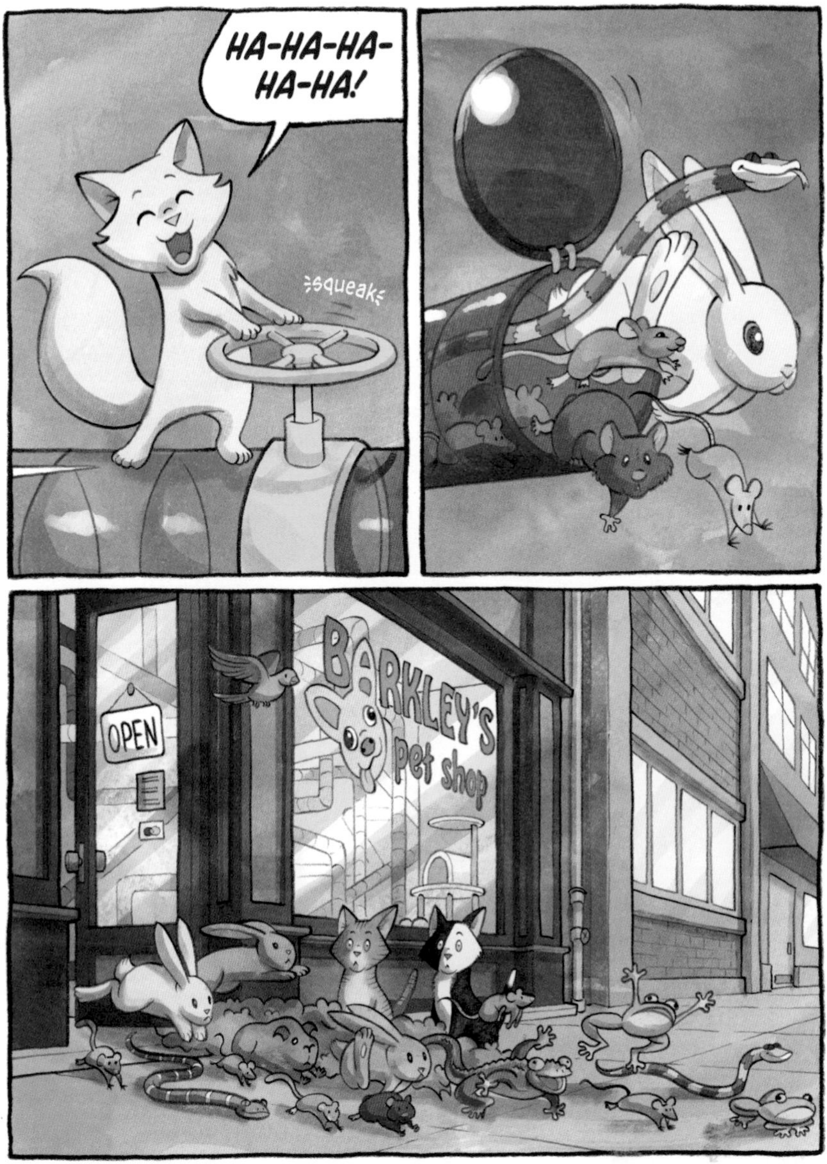
HA-HA-HA-
HA-HA!
squeak
OPEN
BARKLEY'S
pet shop

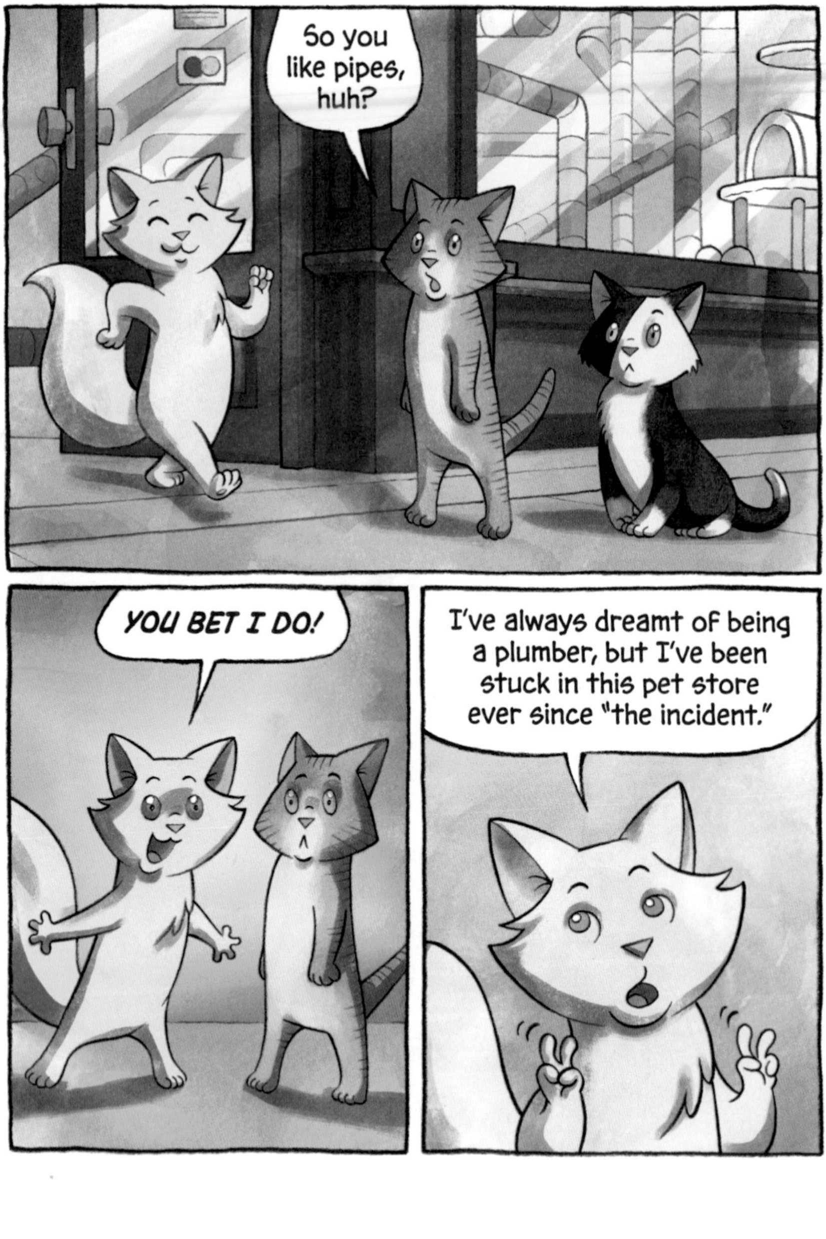
So you like pipes, huh?
YOU BET I DO!
I've always dreamt of being a plumber, but I've been stuck in this pet store ever since "the incident."

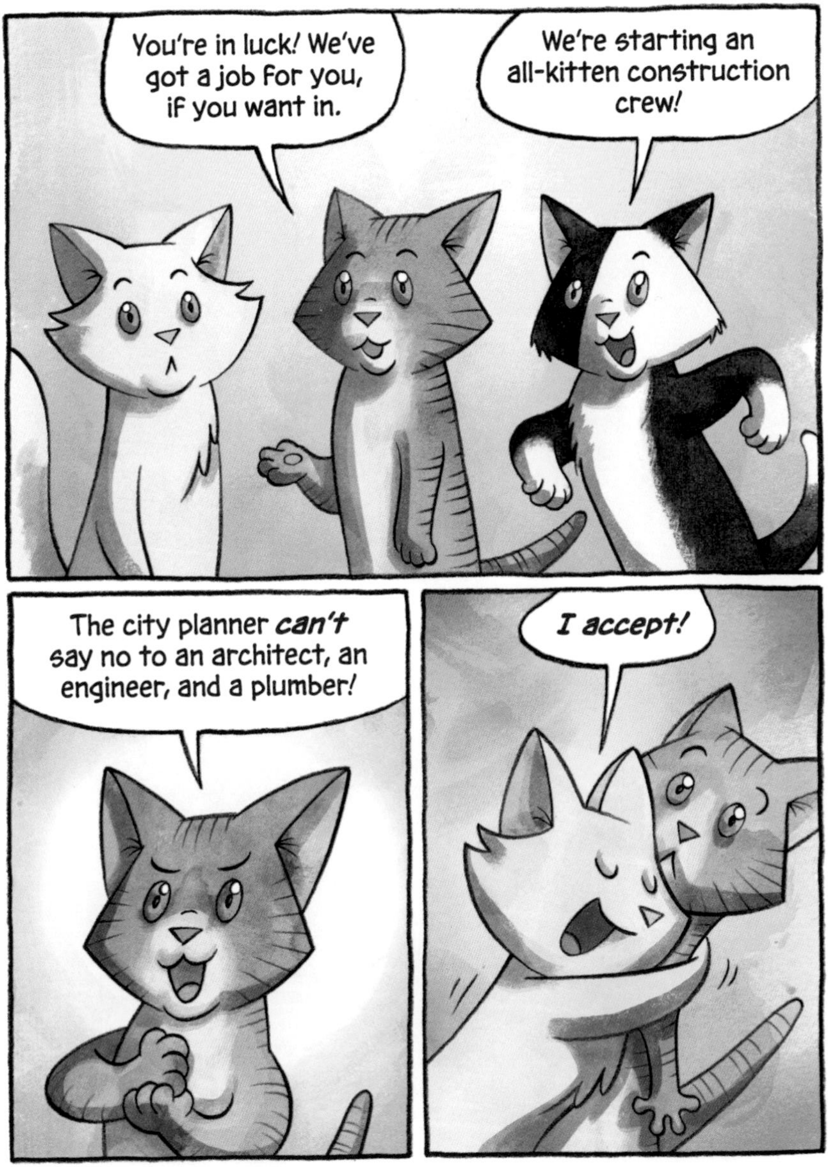
You're in luck! We've got a job for you, if you want in.
We're starting an all-kitten construction crew!
The city planner *can't* say no to an architect, an engineer, and a plumber!
I accept!

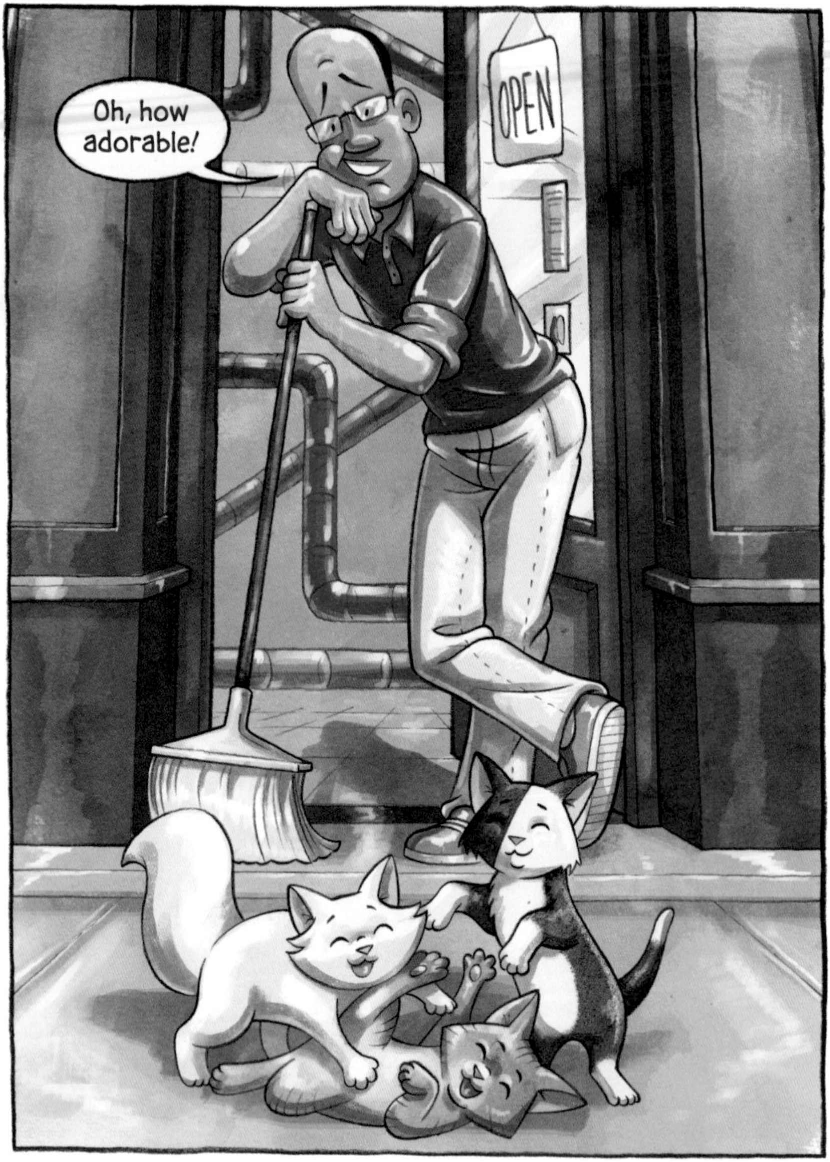
Oh, how adorable!
OPEN

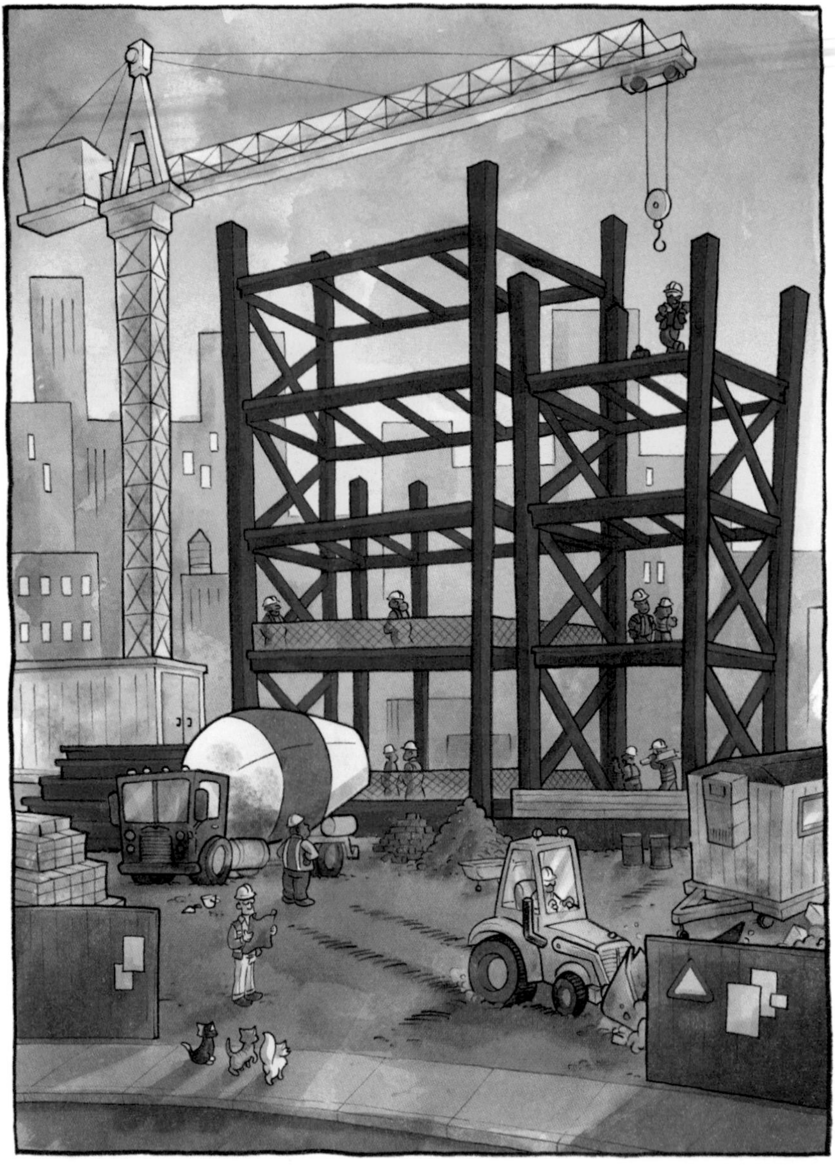

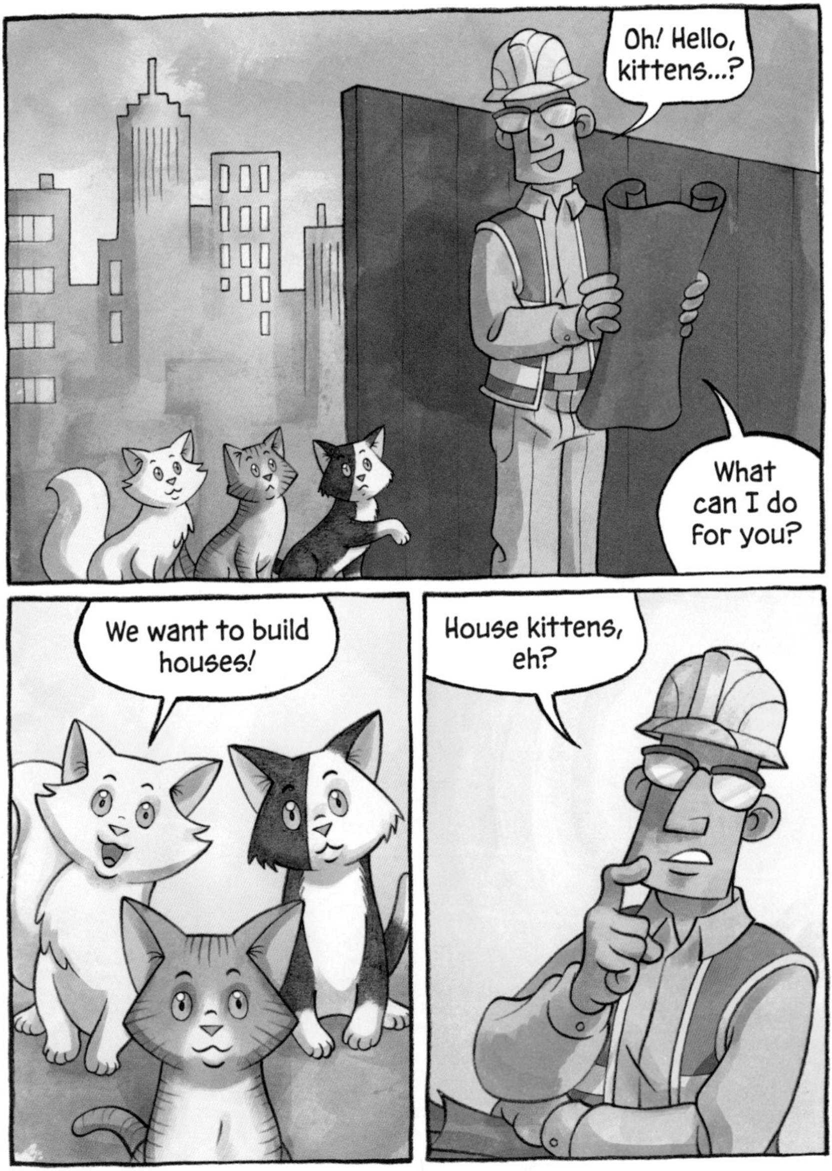
Oh! Hello, kittens...?
What can I do for you?
We want to build houses!
House kittens, eh?

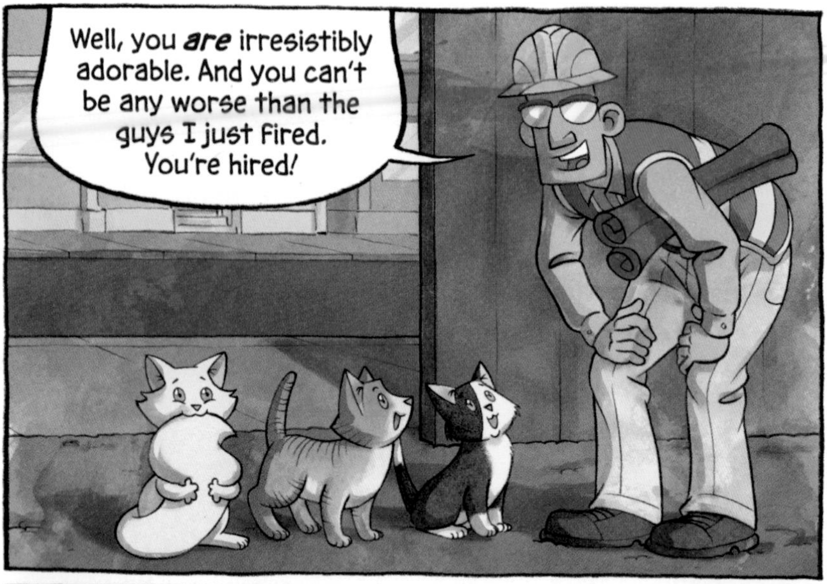
Well, you *are* irresistibly adorable. And you can't be any worse than the guys I just fired. You're hired!

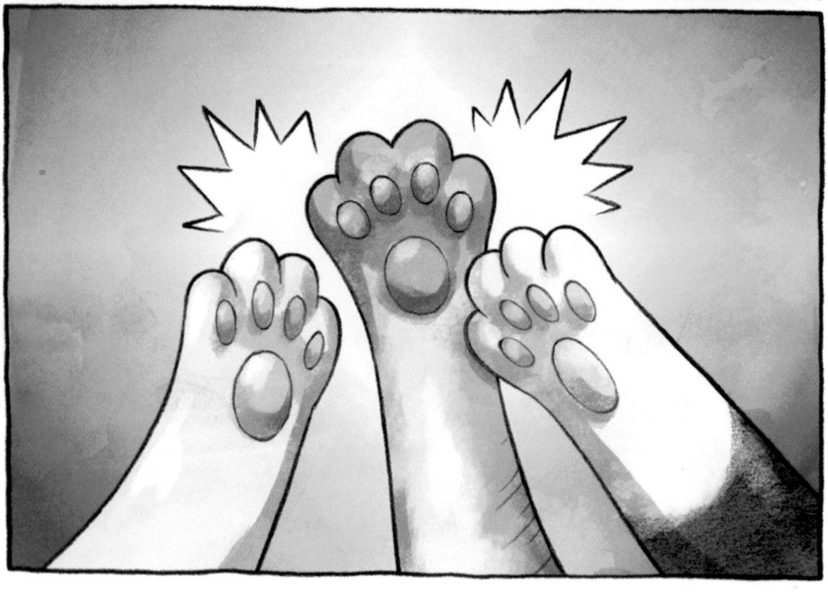

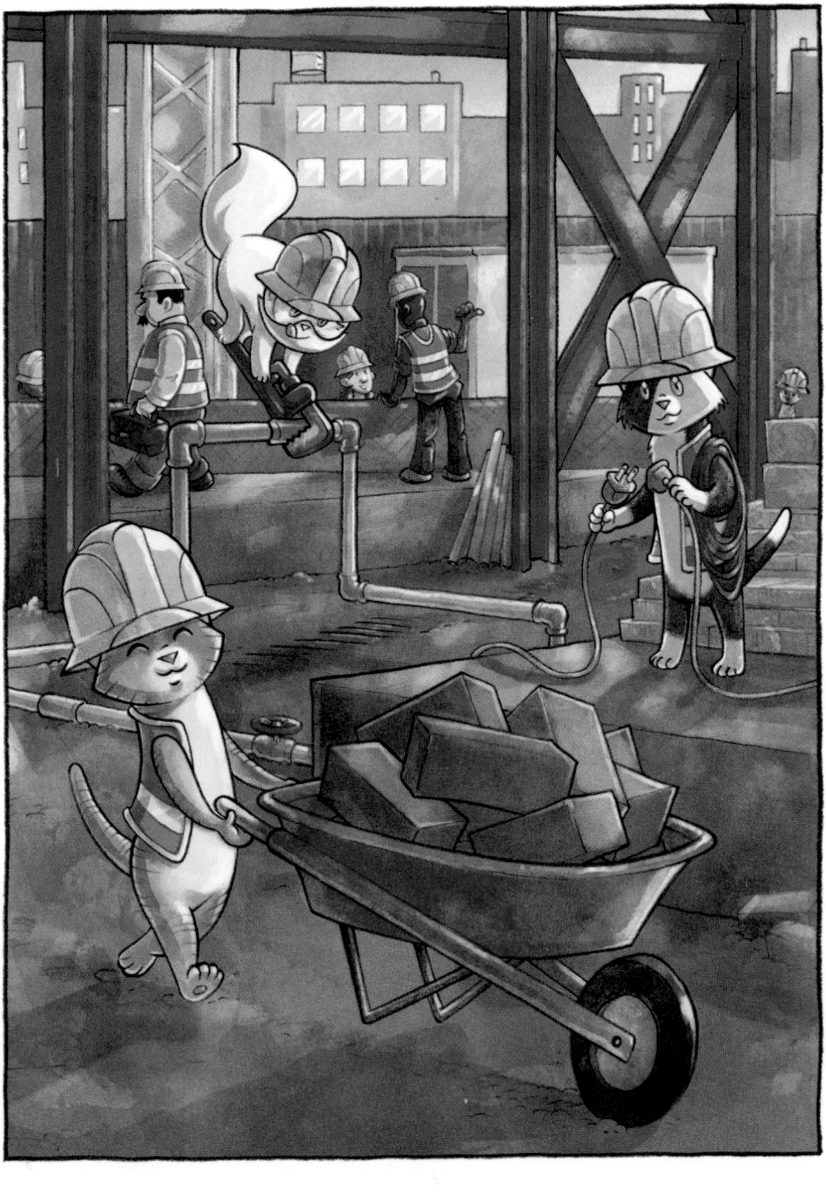

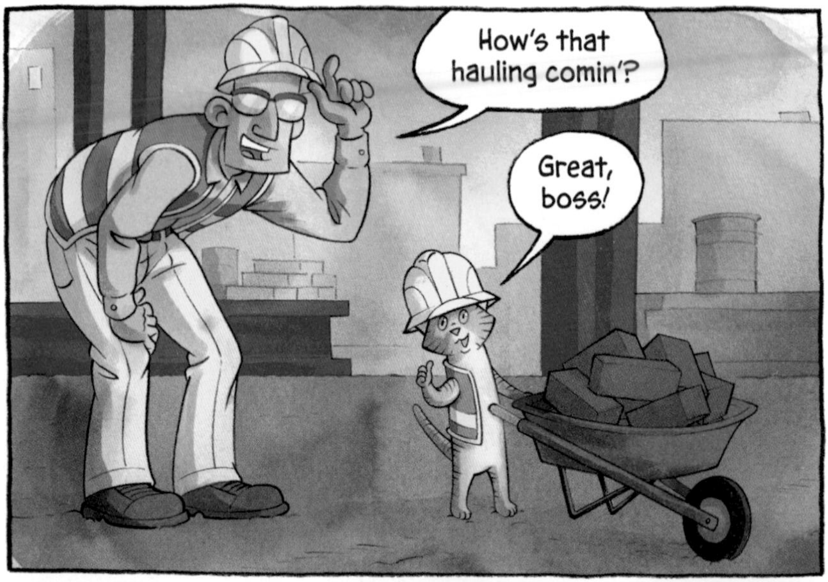
How's that hauling comin'?
Great, boss!
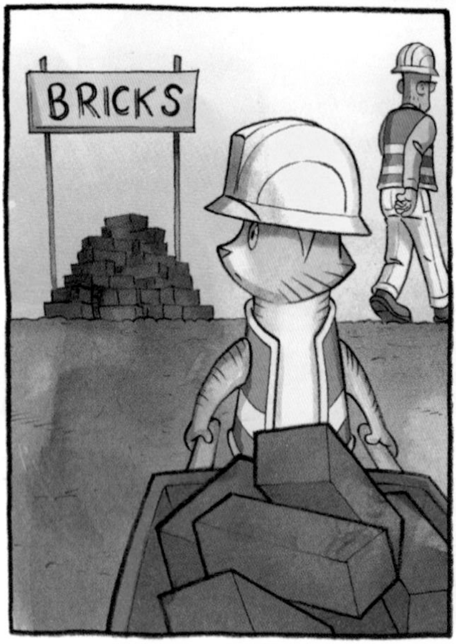
BRICKS
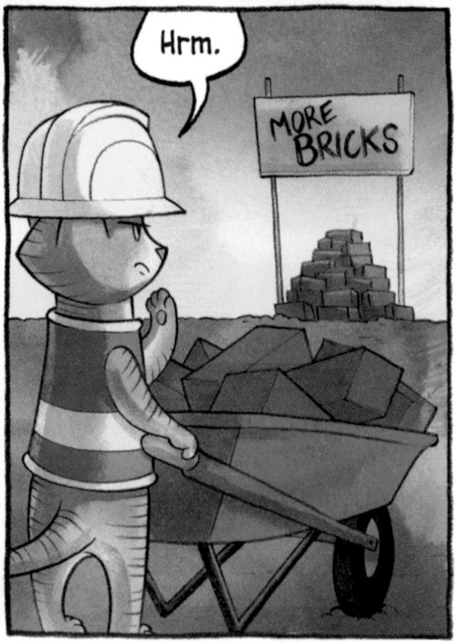
Hrm.
MORE BRICKS

31

32

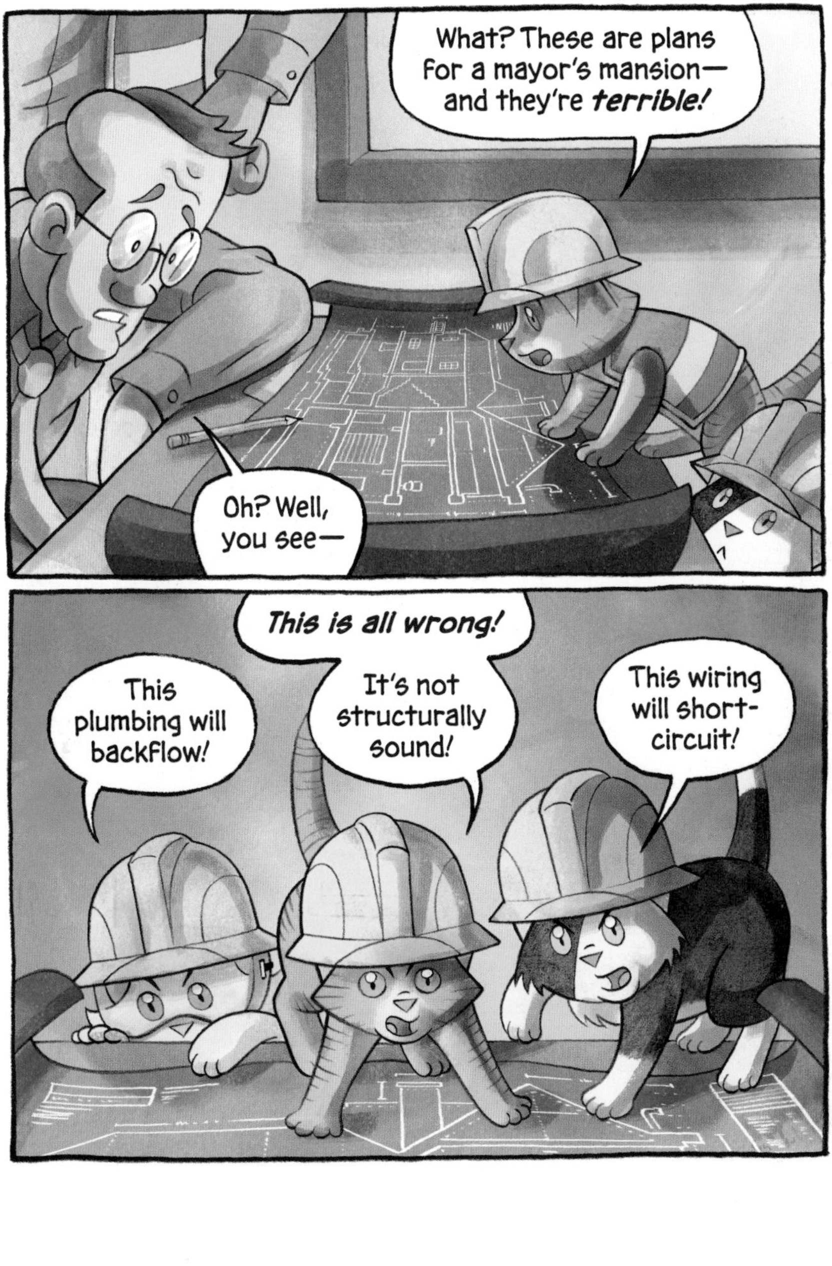
What? These are plans for a mayor's mansion—and they're ***terrible!***
Oh? Well, you see—
This is all wrong!
This plumbing will backflow!
It's not structurally sound!
This wiring will short-circuit!

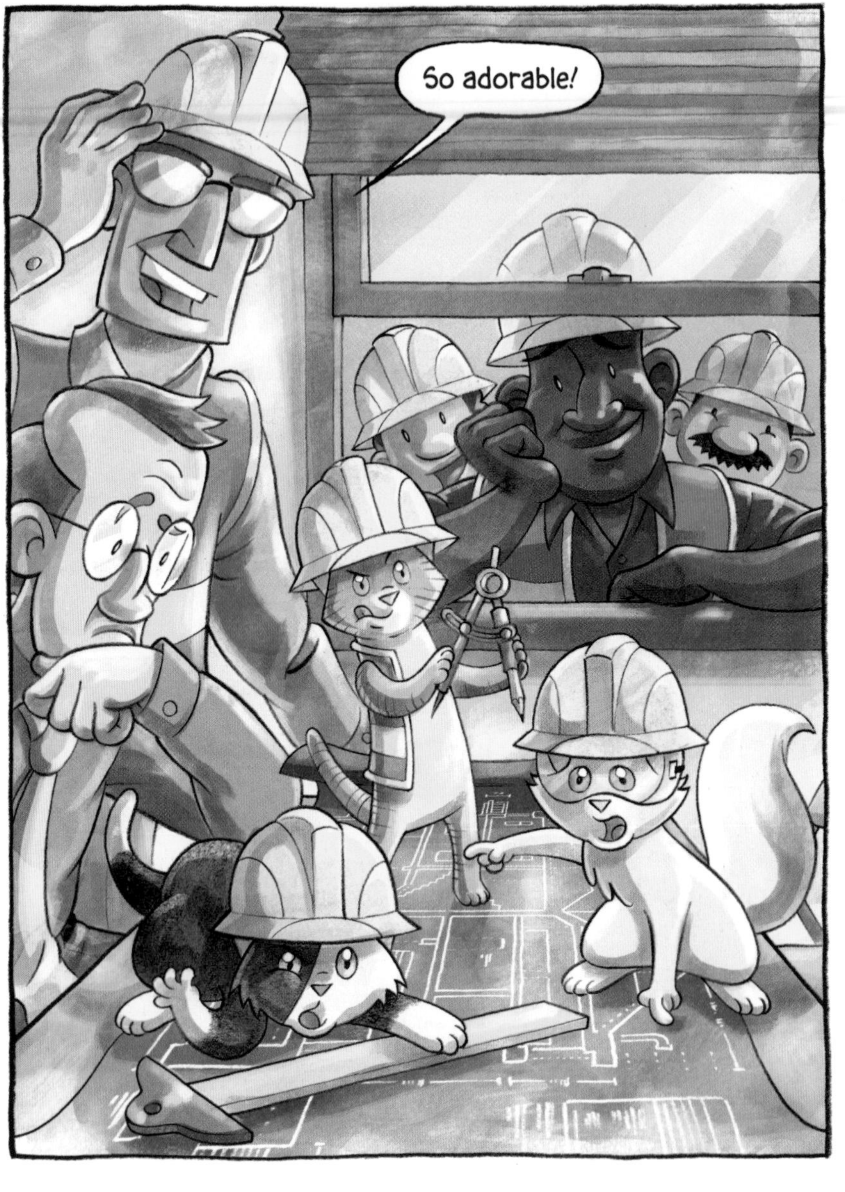
So adorable!

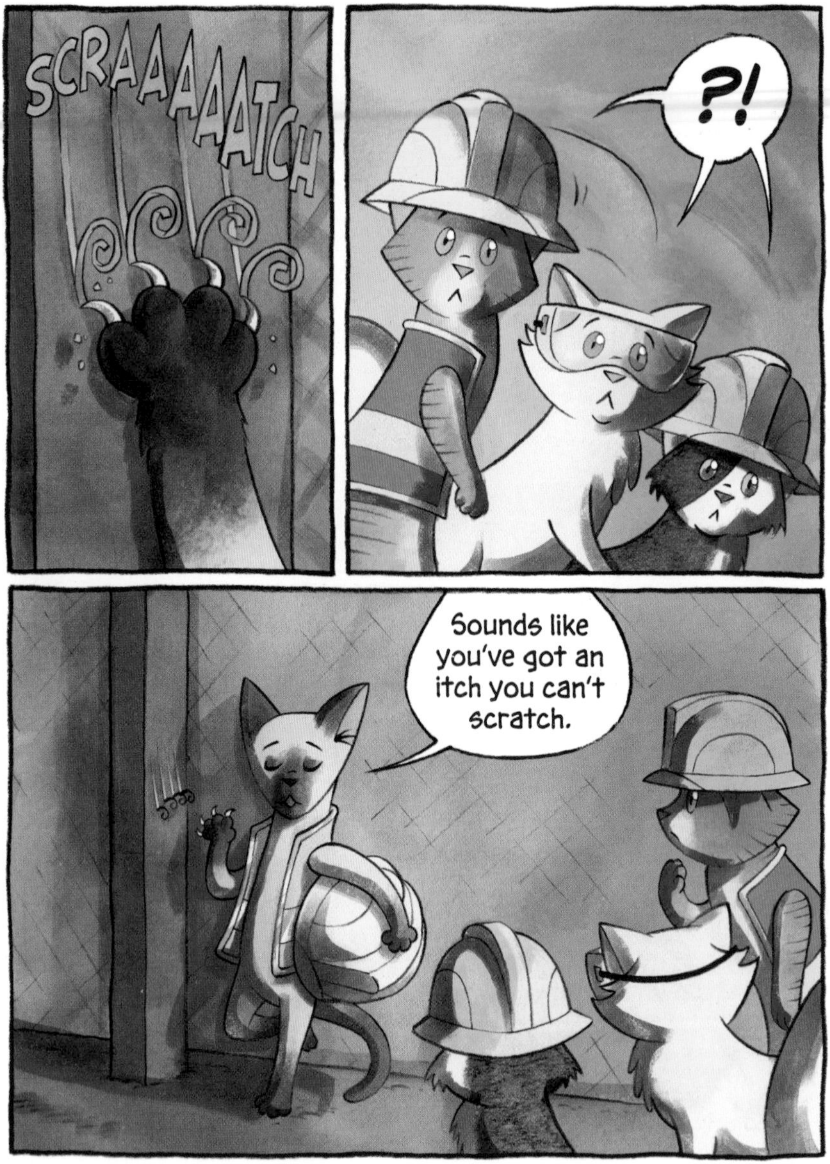
SCRAAAAAATCH
?!
Sounds like you've got an itch you can't scratch.

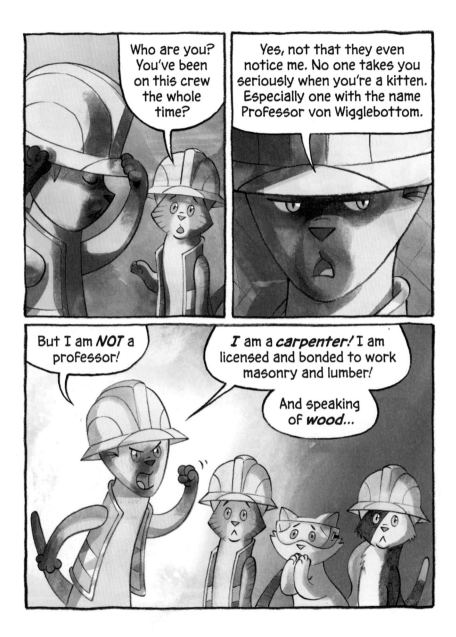

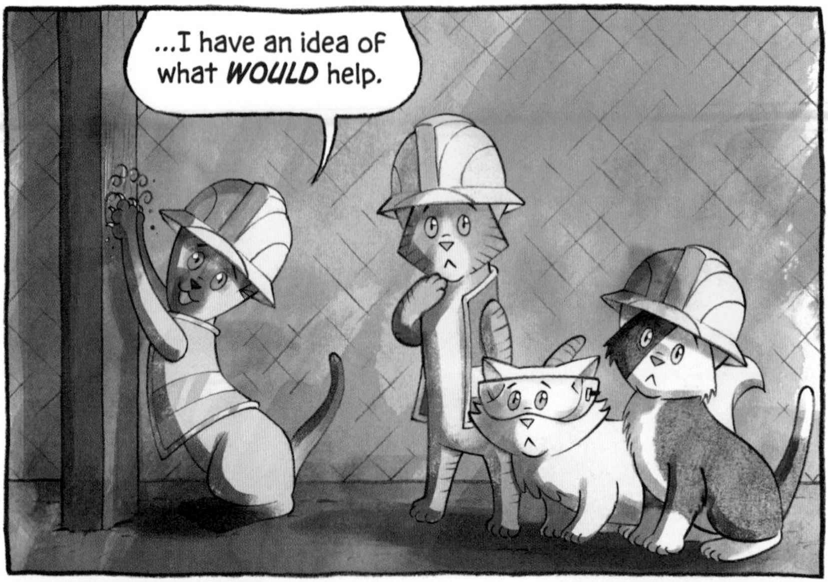
...I have an idea of
what ***WOULD*** help.

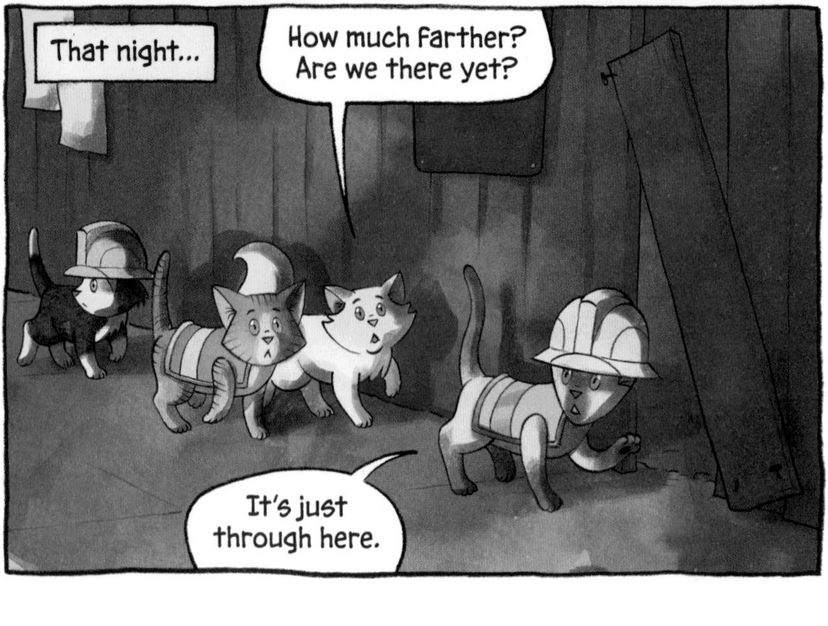
That night...
How much farther?
Are we there yet?
It's just
through here.

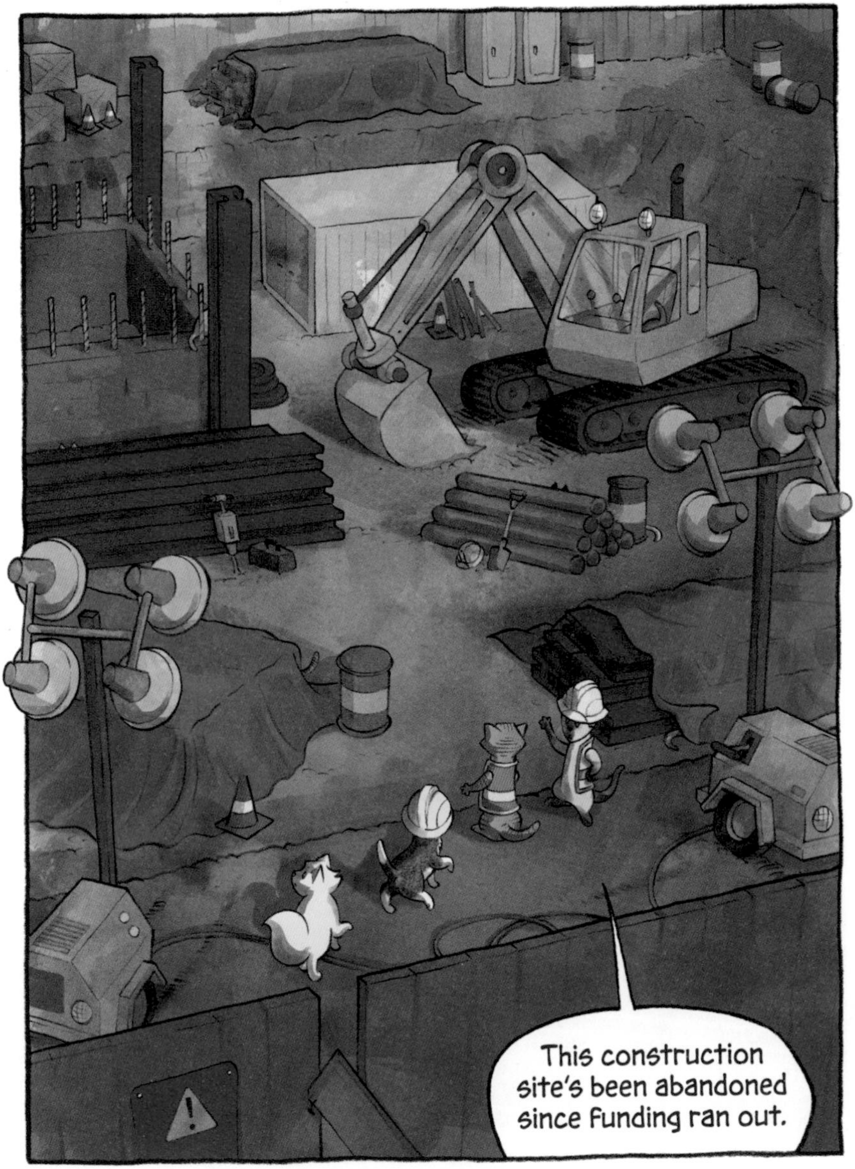
This construction site's been abandoned since funding ran out.

40

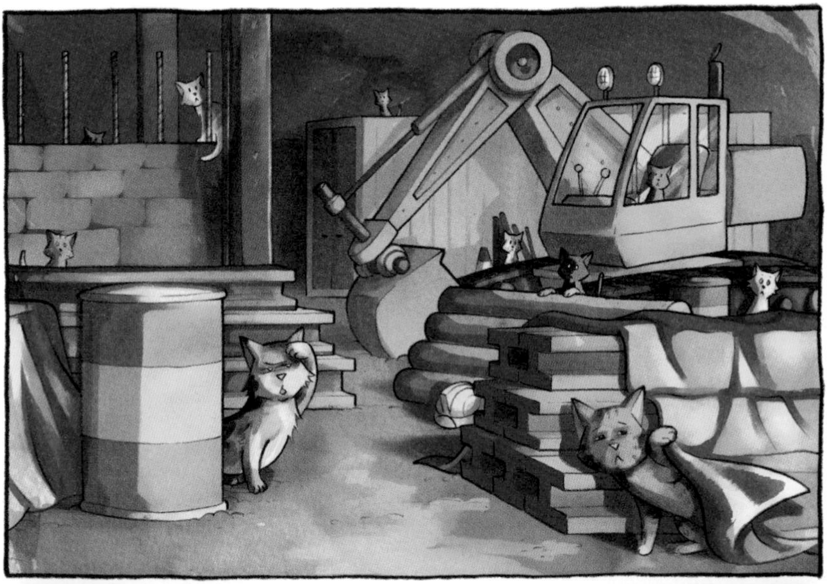

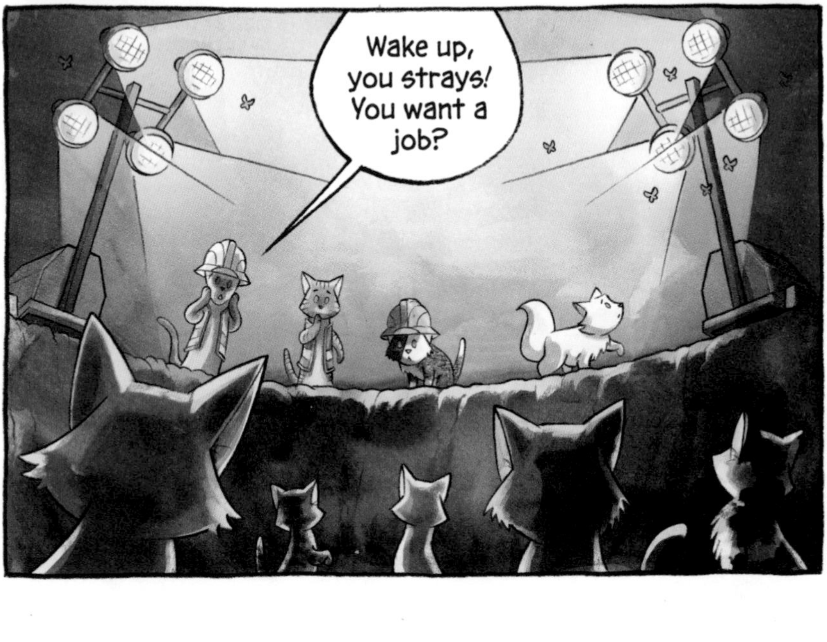
Wake up, you strays! You want a job?

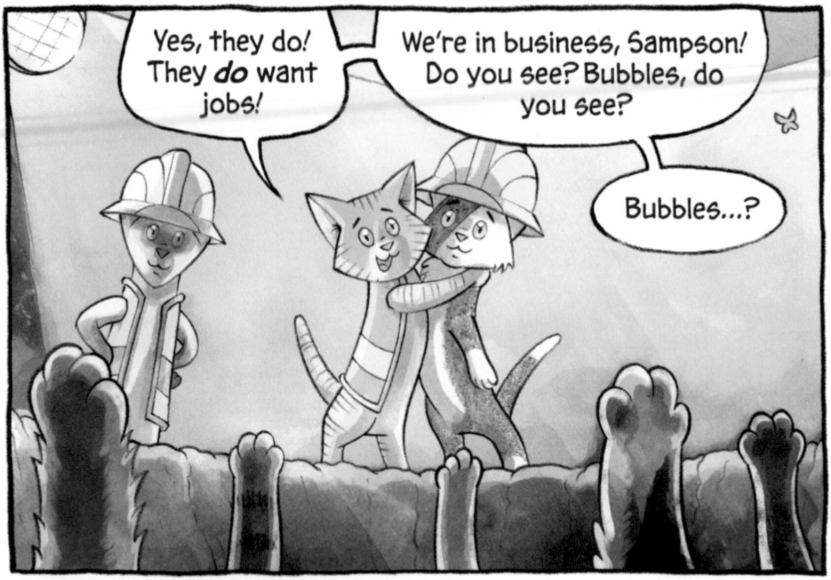
Yes, they do! They *do* want jobs!
We're in business, Sampson! Do you see? Bubbles, do you see?
Bubbles...?

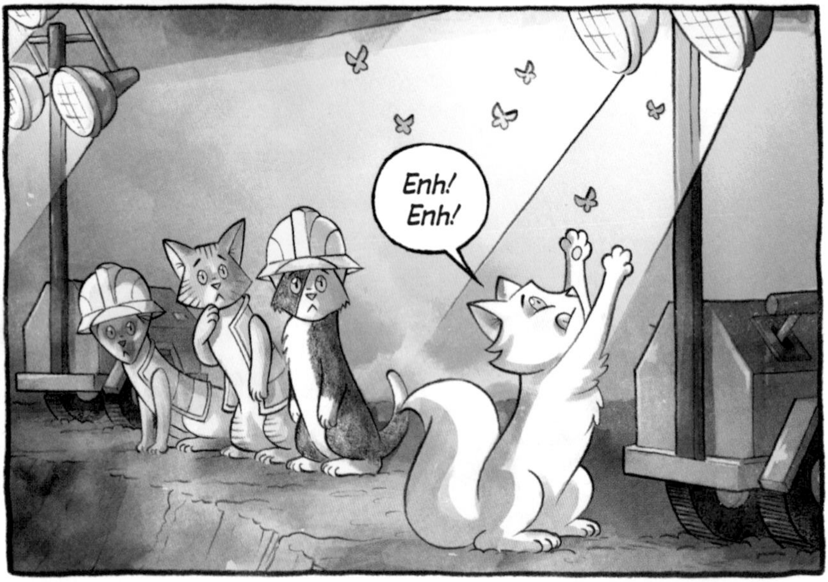
Enh! Enh!

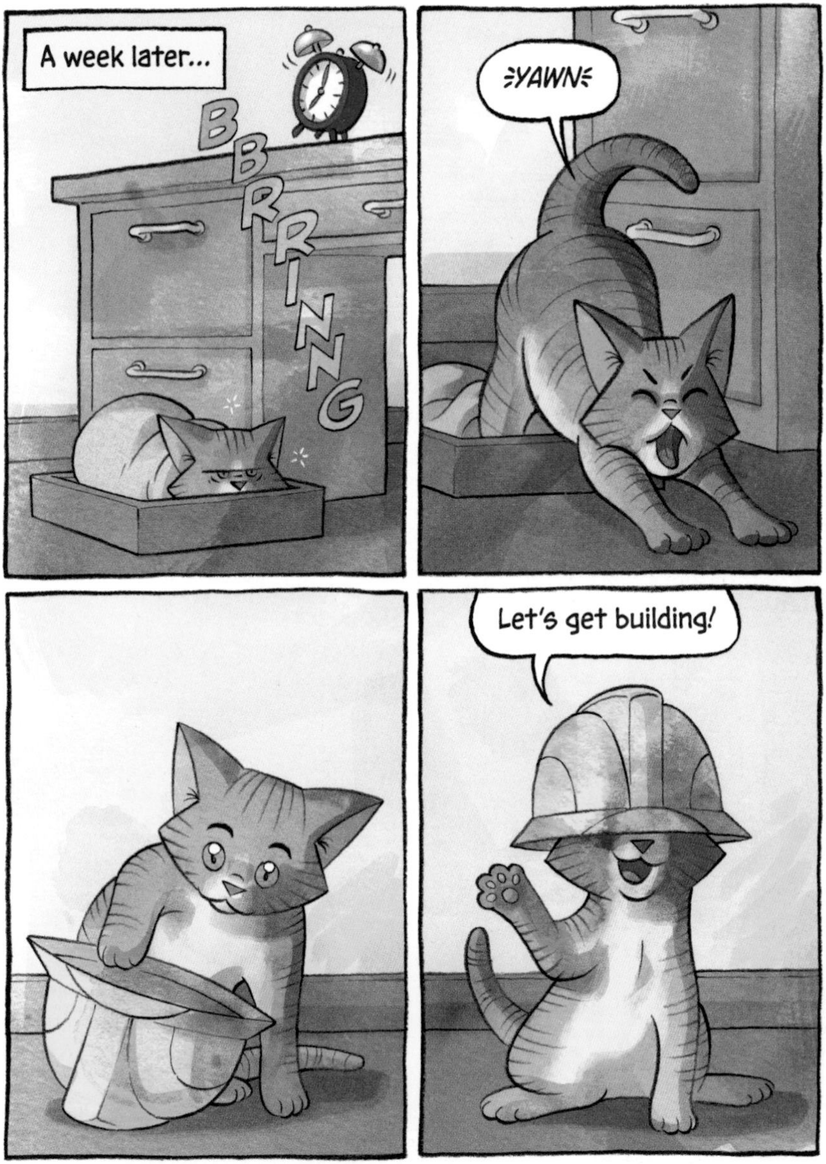
A week later...
BBRRING
≶YAWN≶
Let's get building!

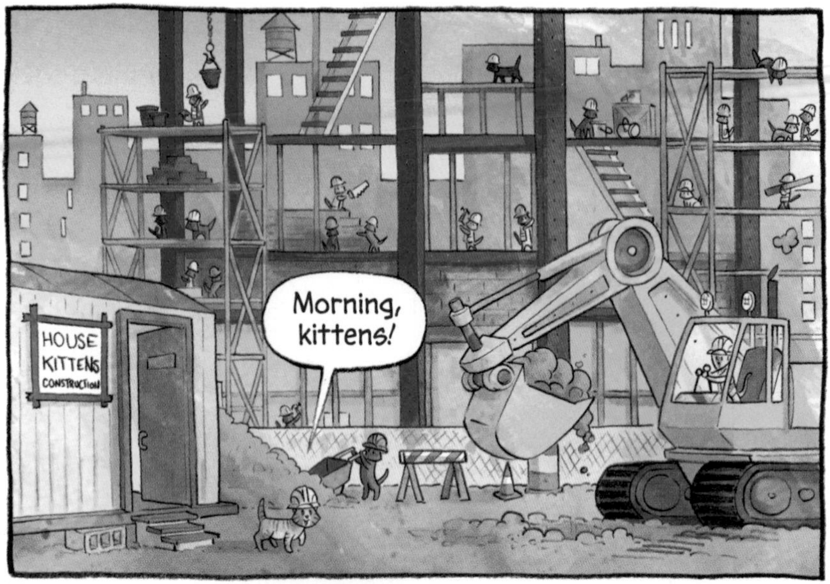
Morning,
kittens!
HOUSE
KITTENS
CONSTRUCTION

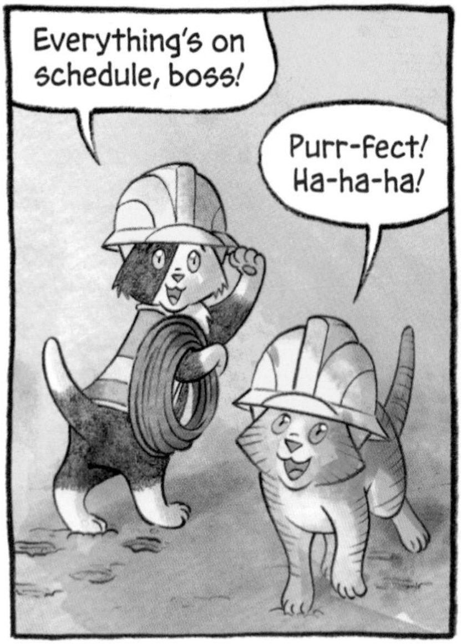
Everything's on
schedule, boss!
Purr-fect!
Ha-ha-ha!

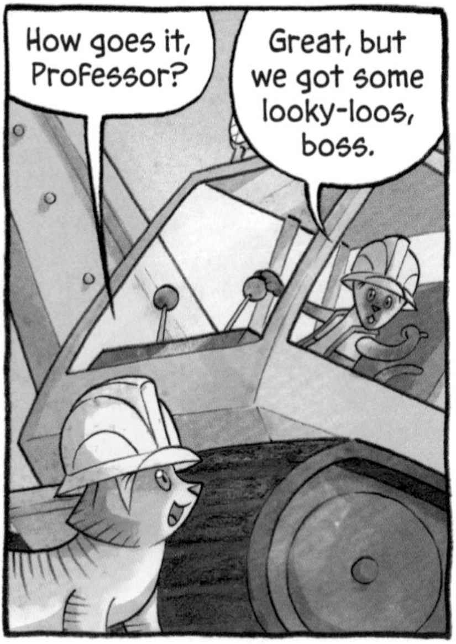
How goes it,
Professor?
Great, but
we got some
looky-loos,
boss.

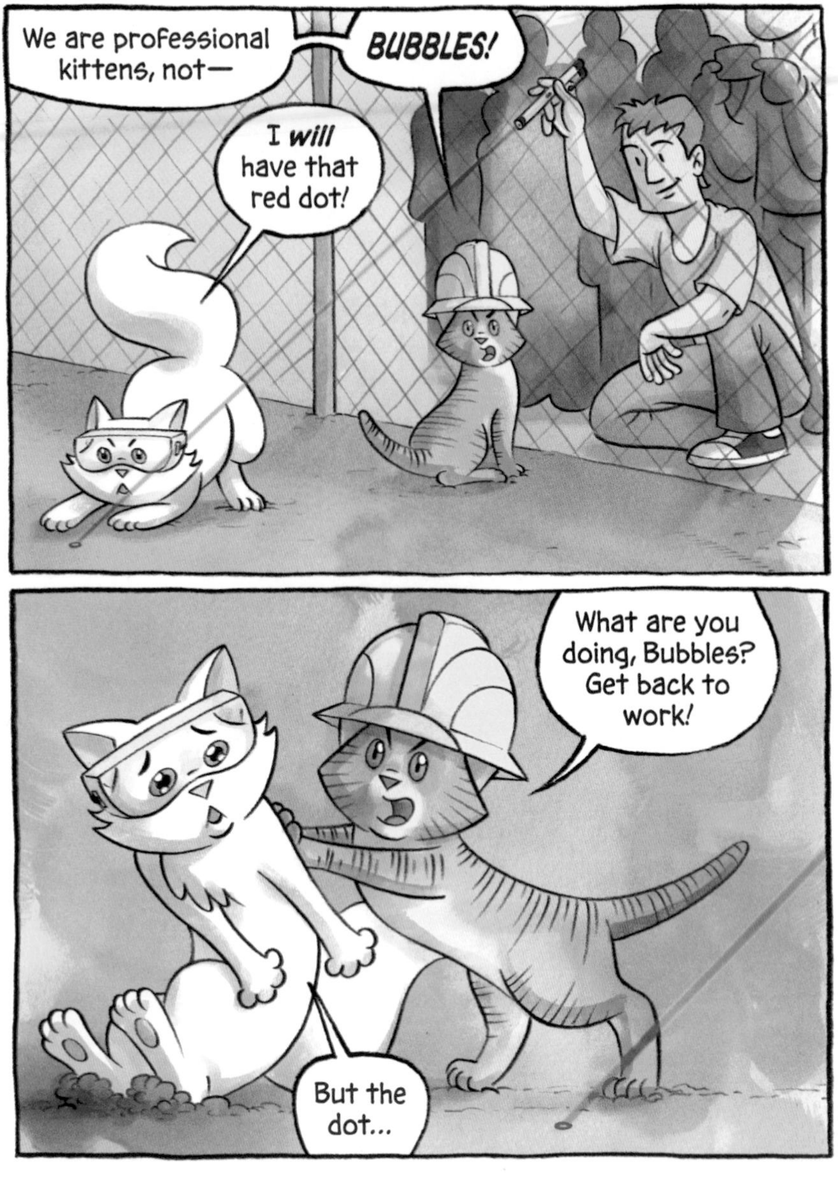
We are professional kittens, not—
BUBBLES!
I *will* have that red dot!
What are you doing, Bubbles? Get back to work!
But the dot...

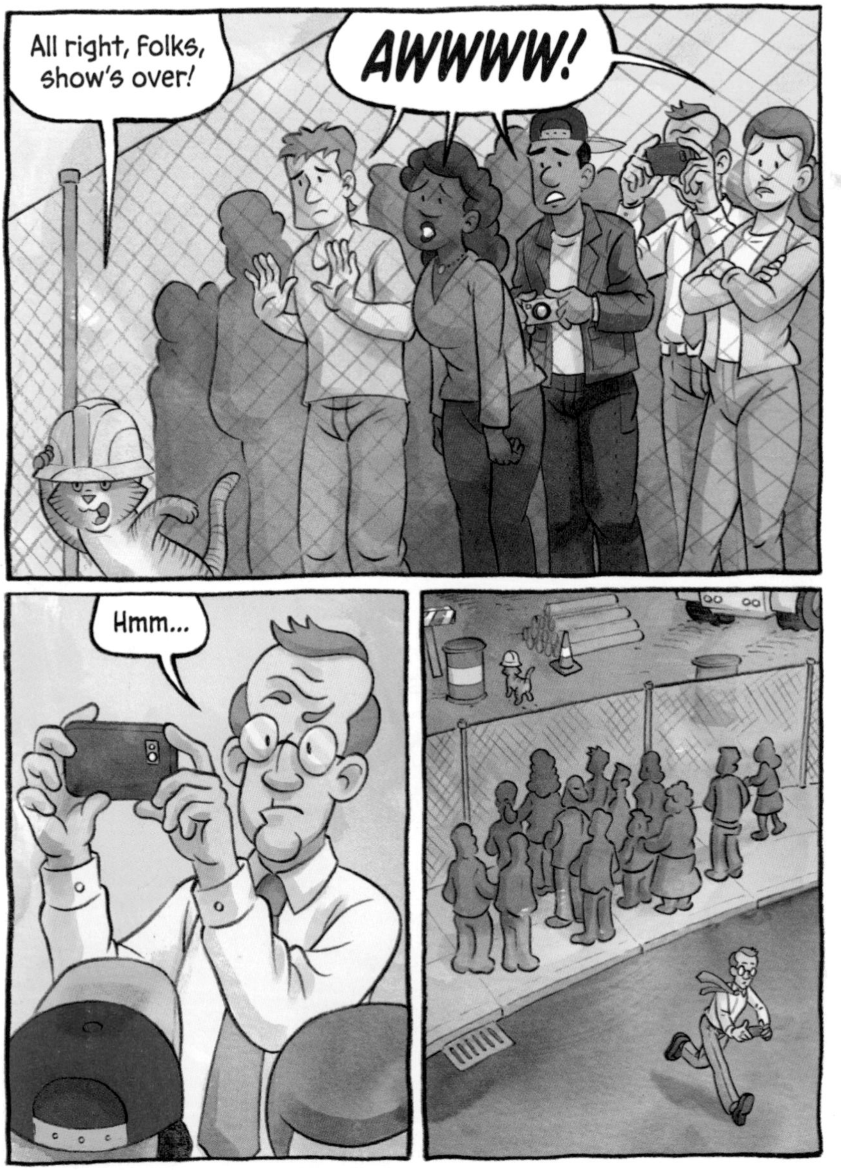
All right, folks, show's over!
AWWWW!
Hmm...

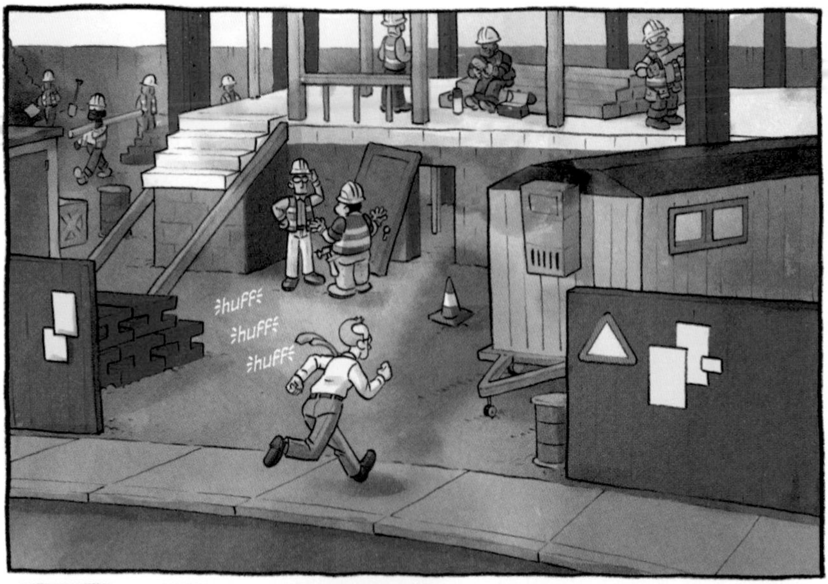
huff
huff
huff

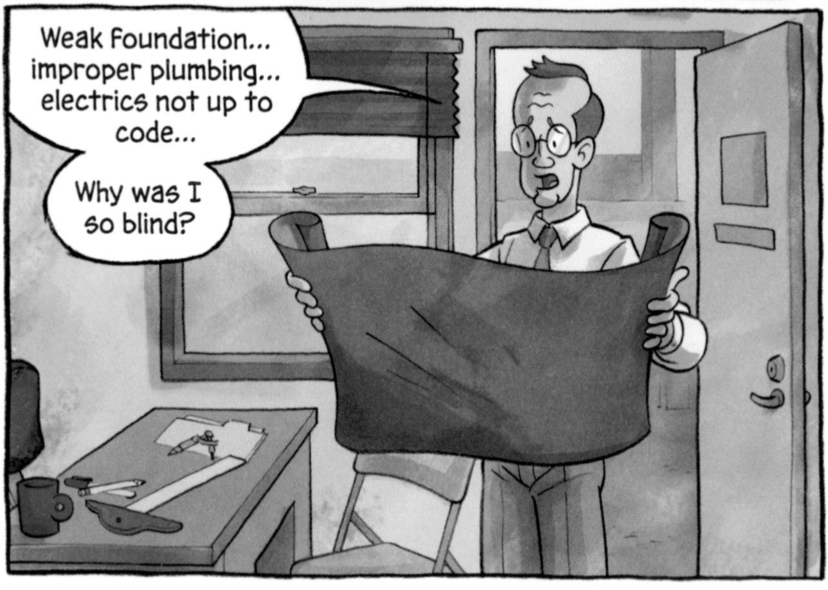
Weak foundation... improper plumbing... electrics not up to code...
Why was I so blind?

49

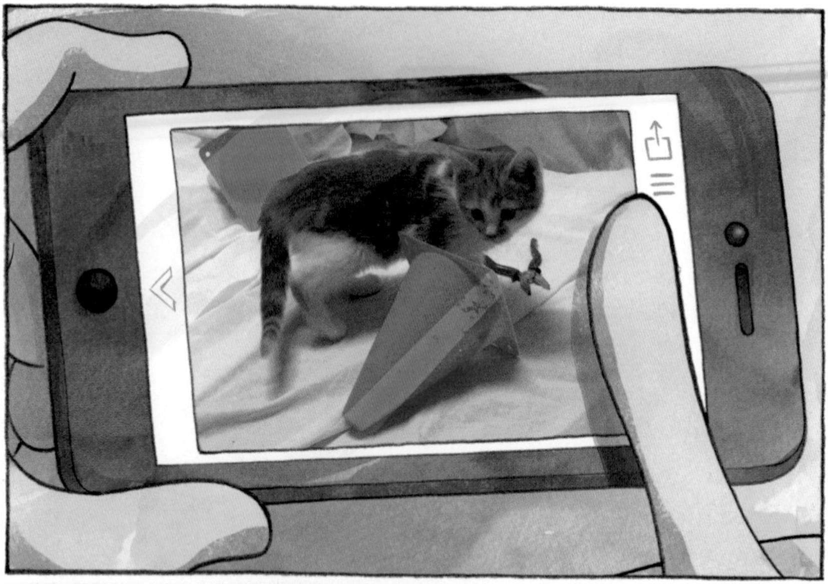
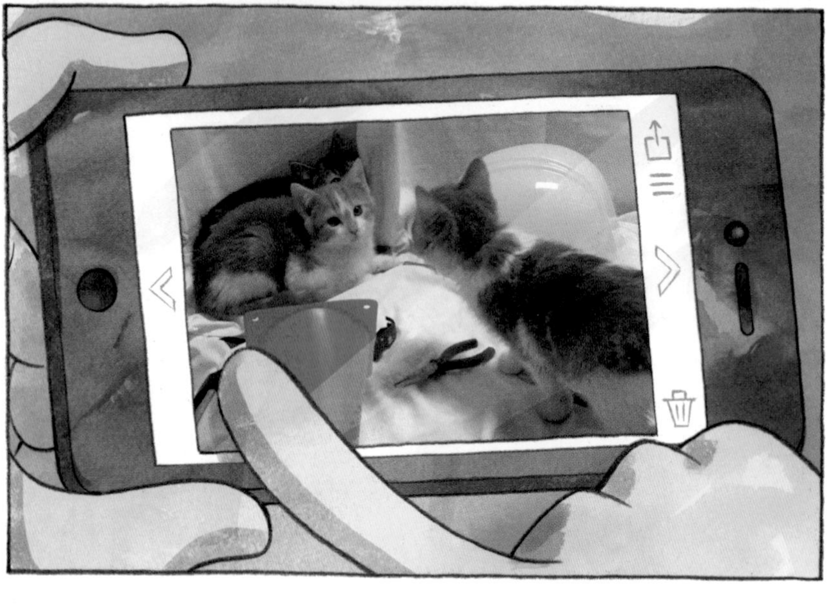

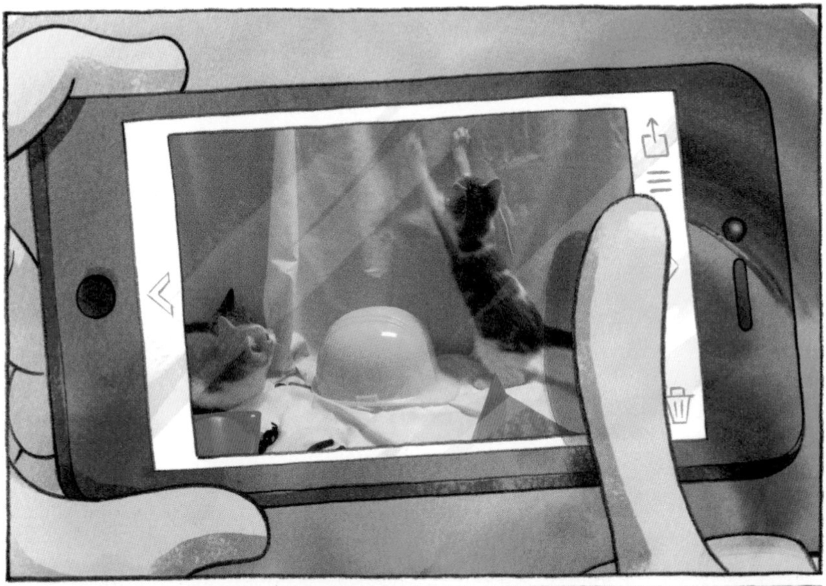

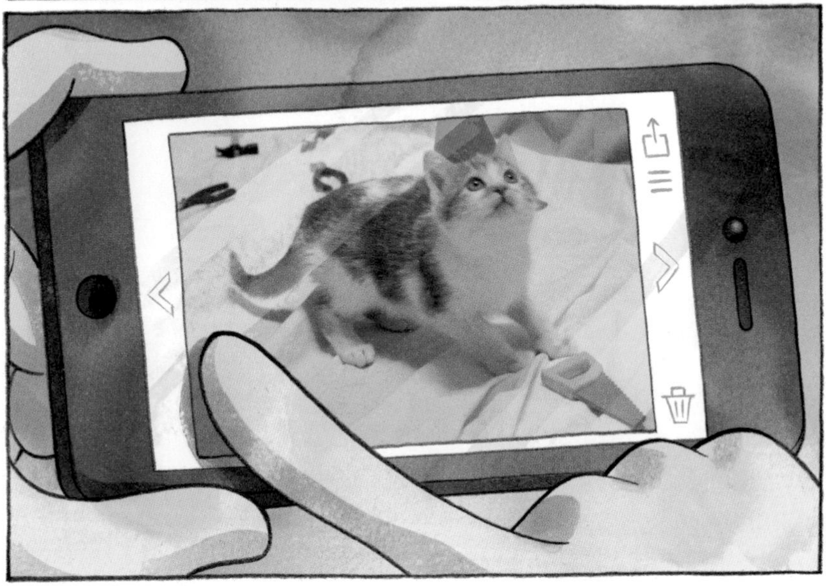

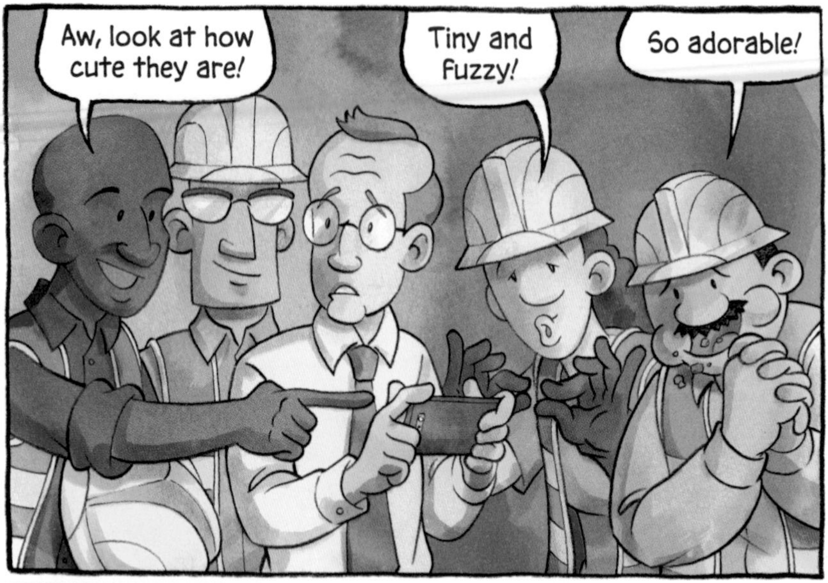
Aw, look at how cute they are!
Tiny and fuzzy!
So adorable!

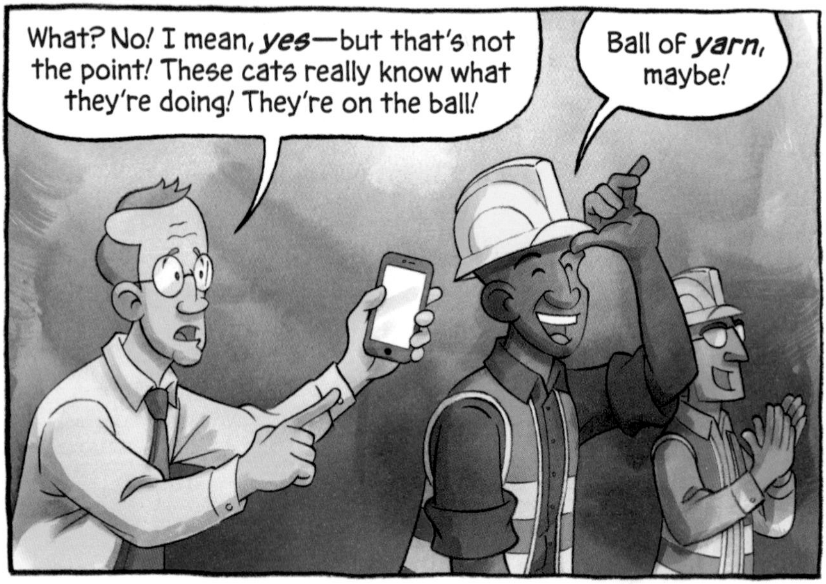
What? No! I mean, ***yes***—but that's not the point! These cats really know what they're doing! They're on the ball!
Ball of ***yarn***, maybe!

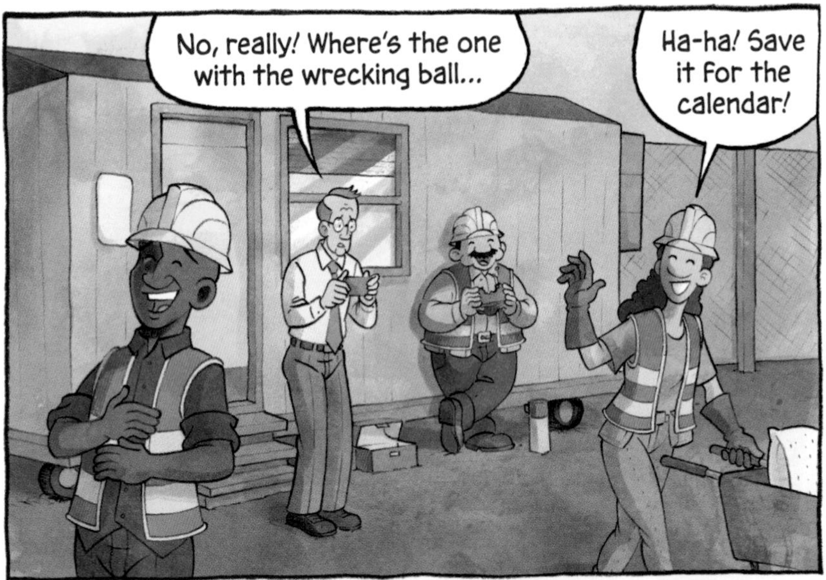
No, really! Where's the one with the wrecking ball...
Ha-ha! Save it for the calendar!

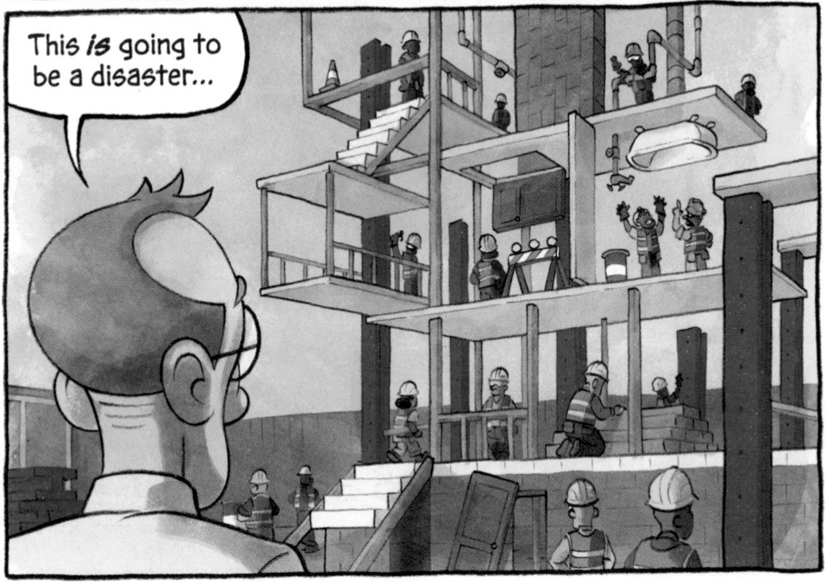
This *is* going to be a disaster...

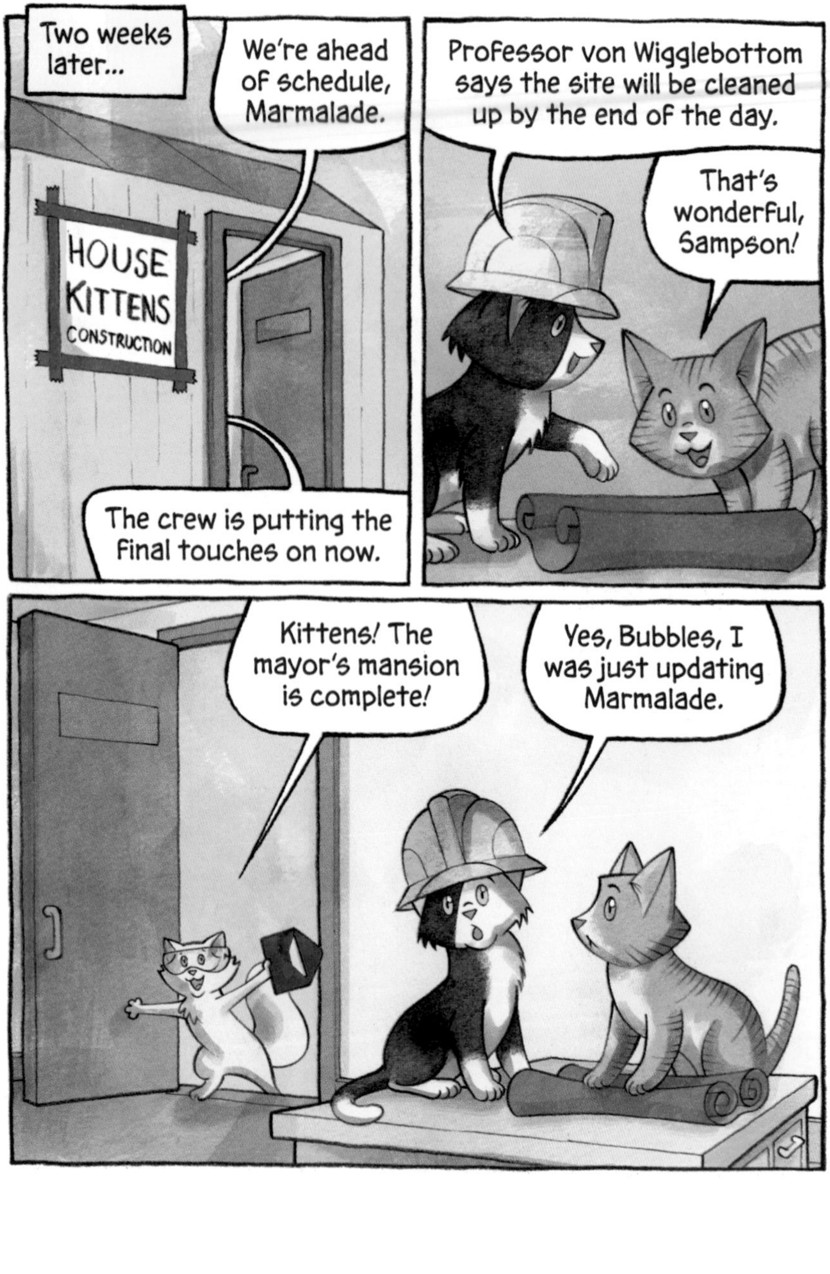
Two weeks later...
We're ahead of schedule, Marmalade.
The crew is putting the final touches on now.
HOUSE KITTENS CONSTRUCTION
Professor von Wigglebottom says the site will be cleaned up by the end of the day.
That's wonderful, Sampson!
Kittens! The mayor's mansion is complete!
Yes, Bubbles, I was just updating Marmalade.

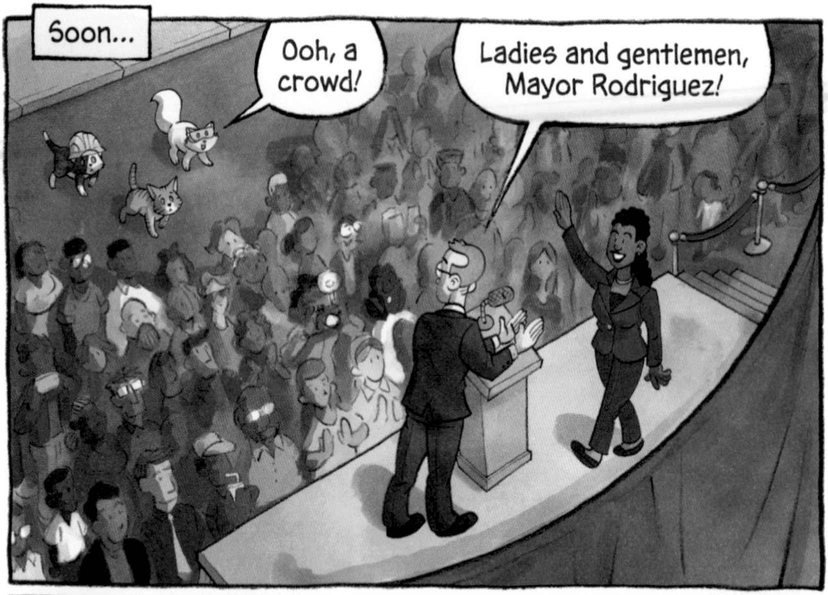
Soon...
Ooh, a crowd!
Ladies and gentlemen, Mayor Rodriguez!

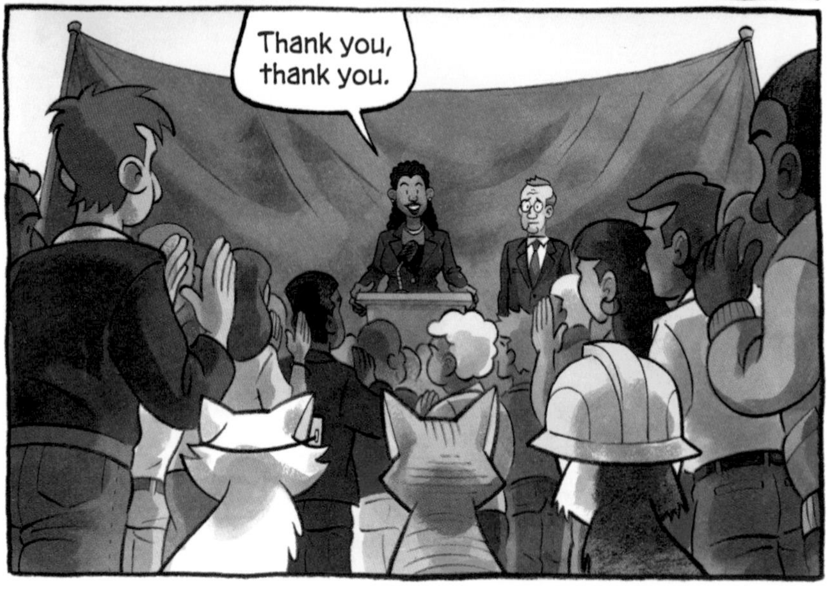
Thank you, thank you.

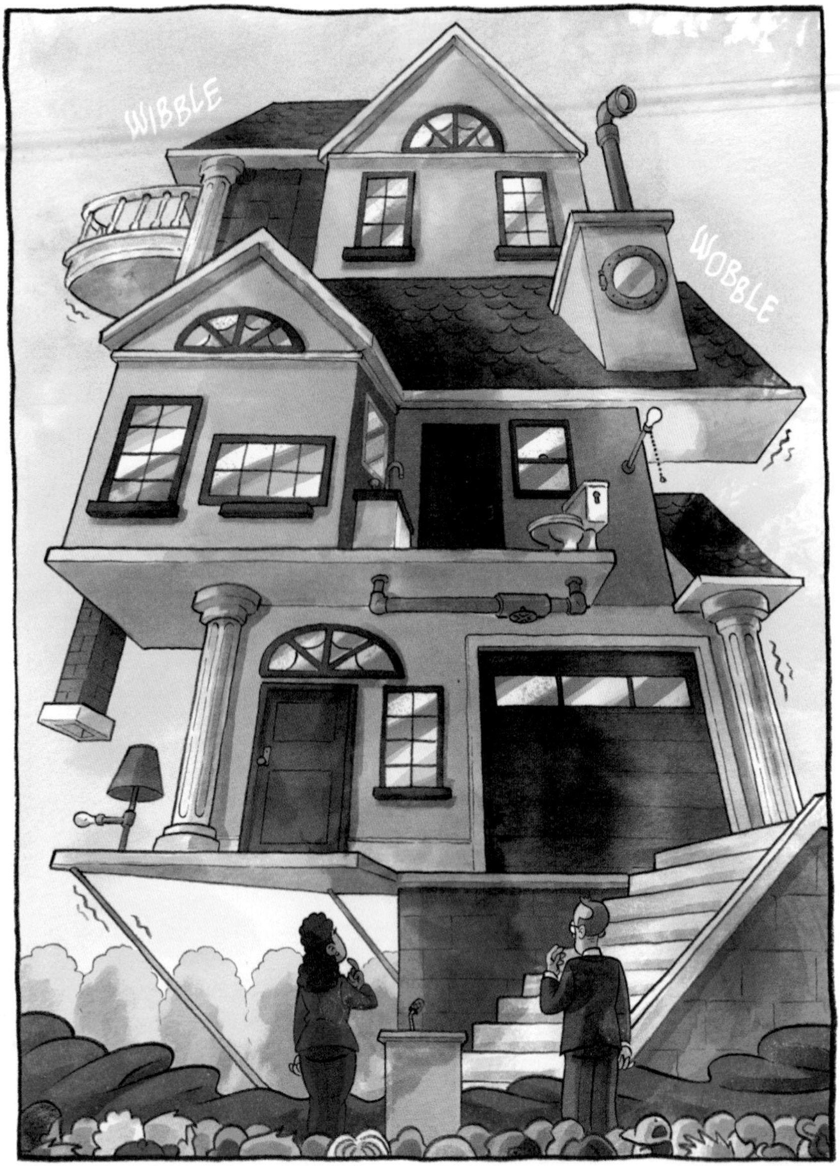
WIBBLE
WOBBLE

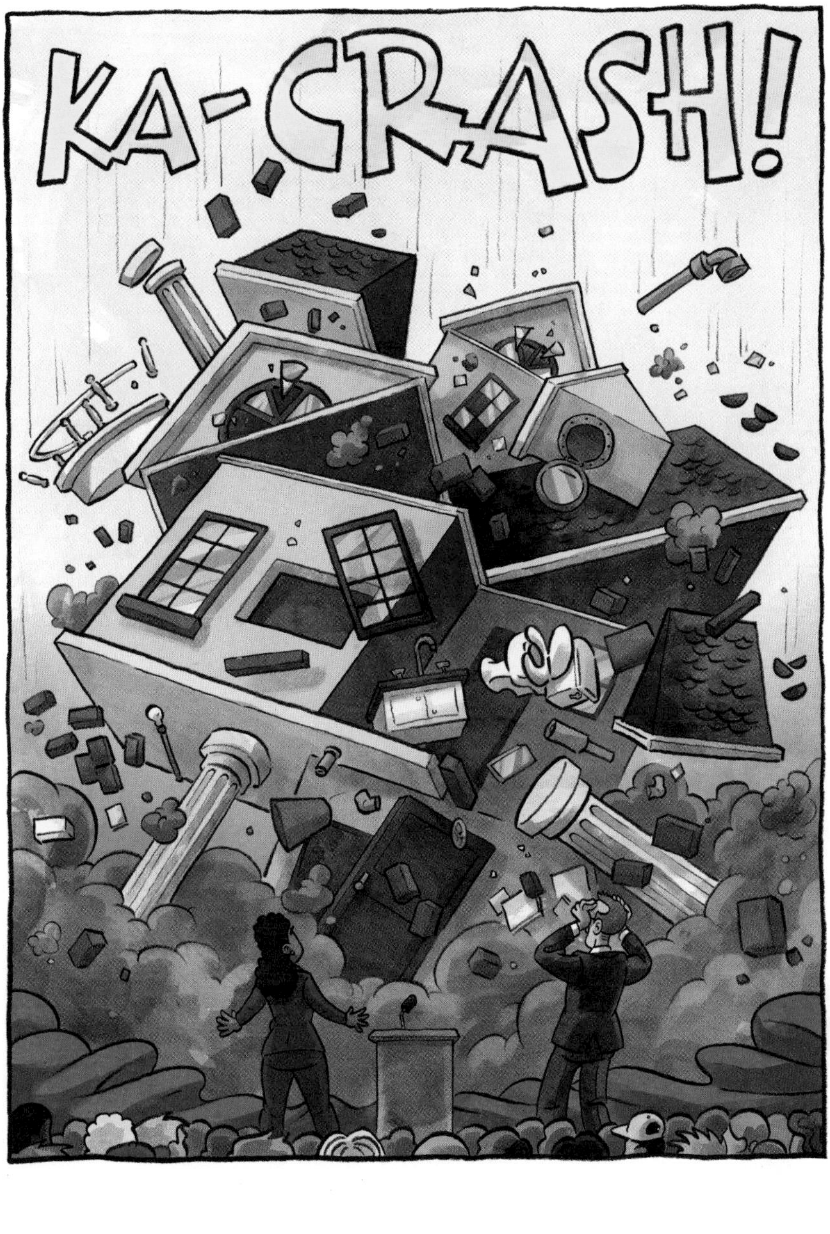
KA-CRASH!

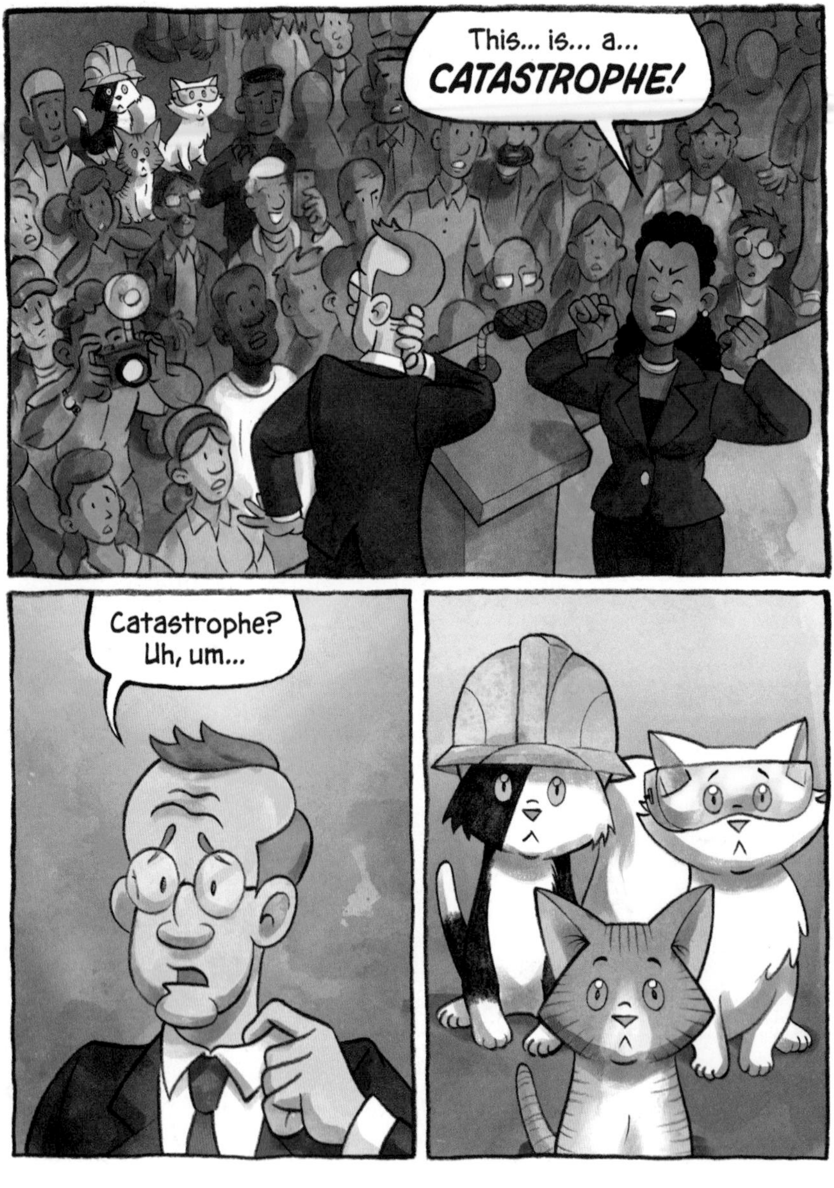
This... is... a... CATASTROPHE!
Catastrophe? Uh, um...

61

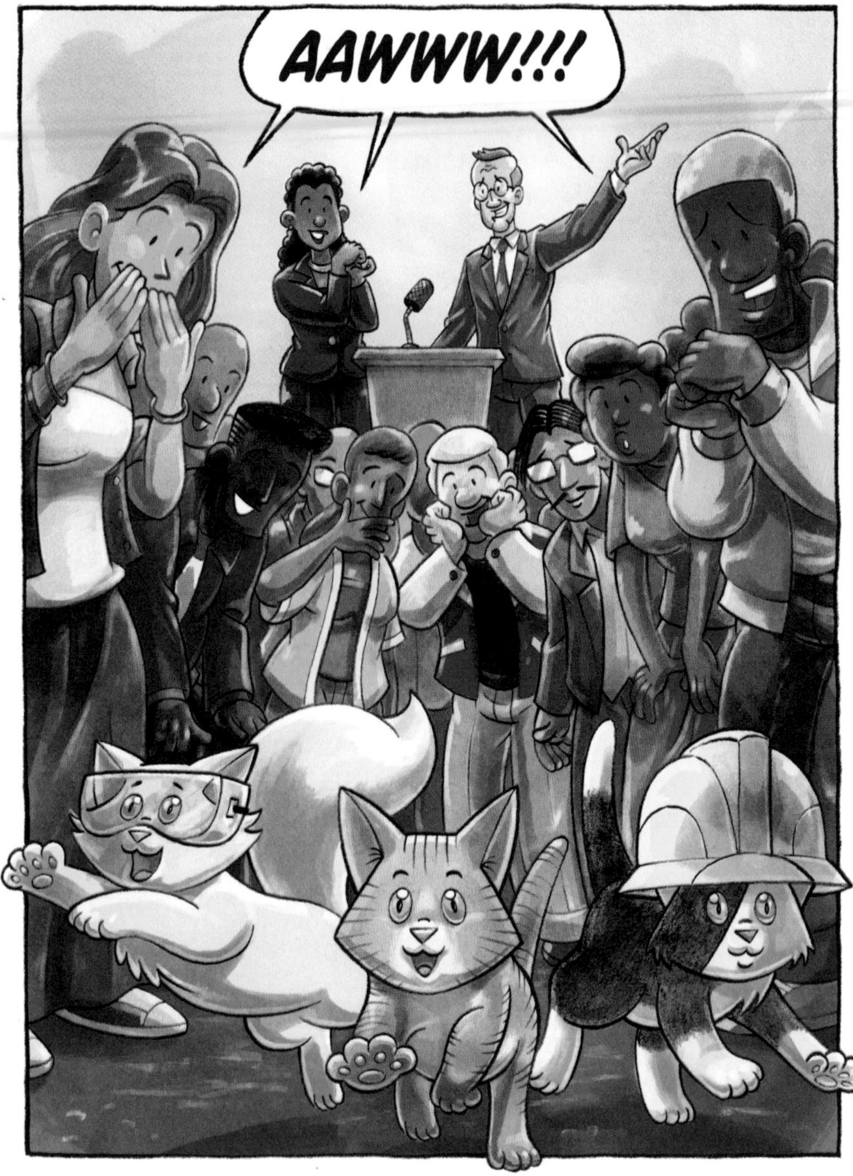
AAWWW!!!

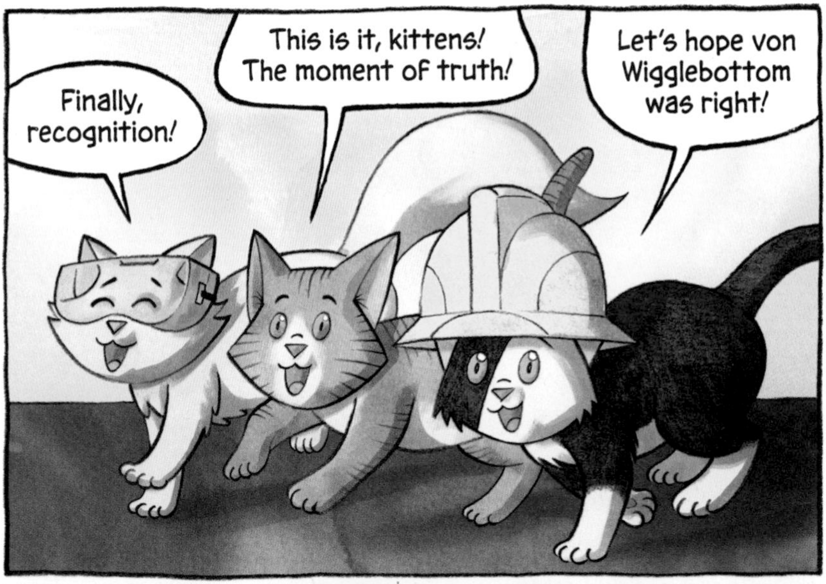
Finally, recognition!
This is it, kittens! The moment of truth!
Let's hope von Wigglebottom was right!

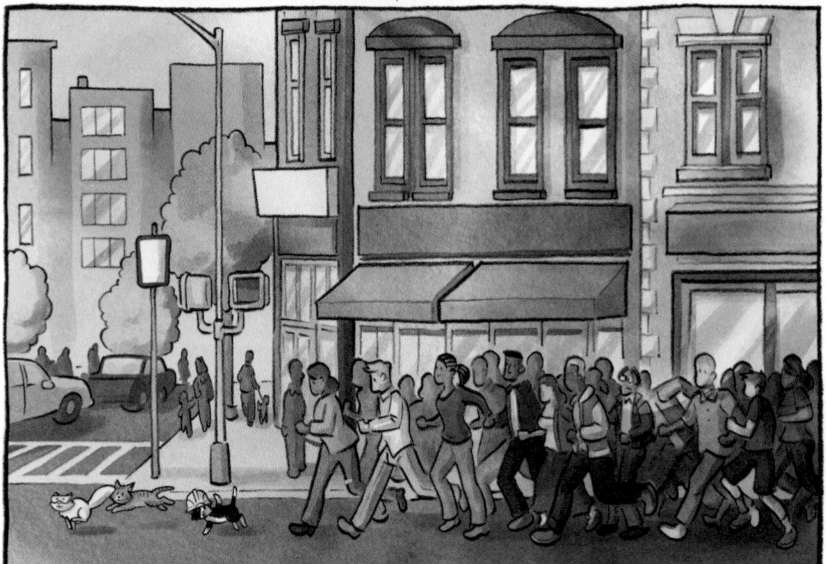

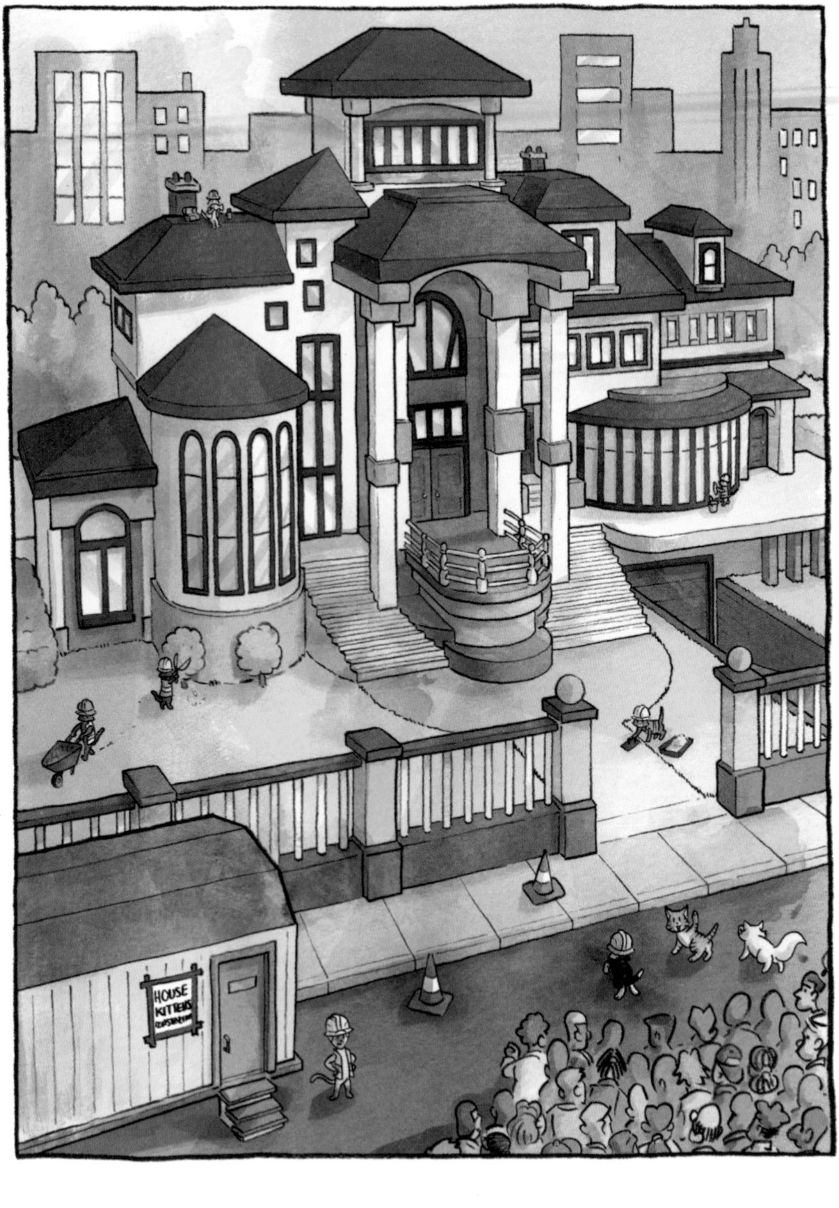
HOUSE
KITTENS

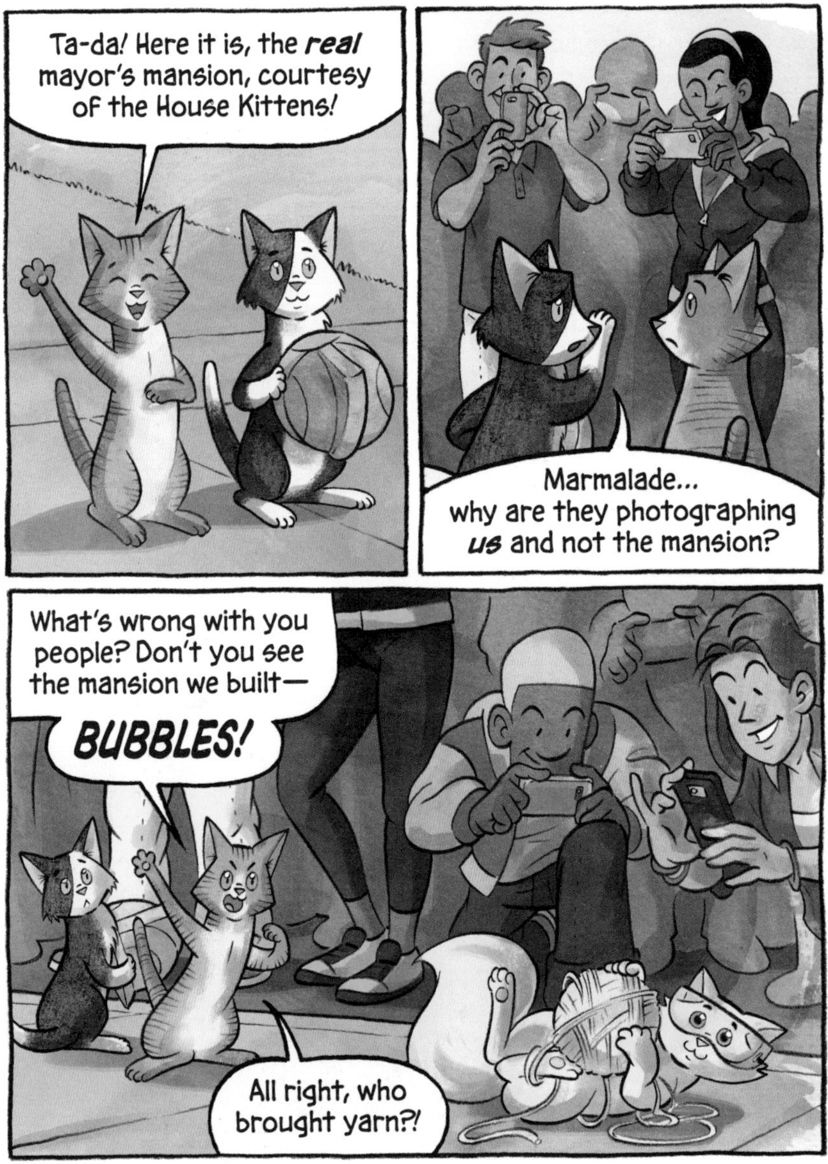
Ta-da! Here it is, the ***real*** mayor's mansion, courtesy of the House Kittens!
Marmalade... why are they photographing ***us*** and not the mansion?
What's wrong with you people? Don't you see the mansion we built—
BUBBLES!
All right, who brought yarn?!

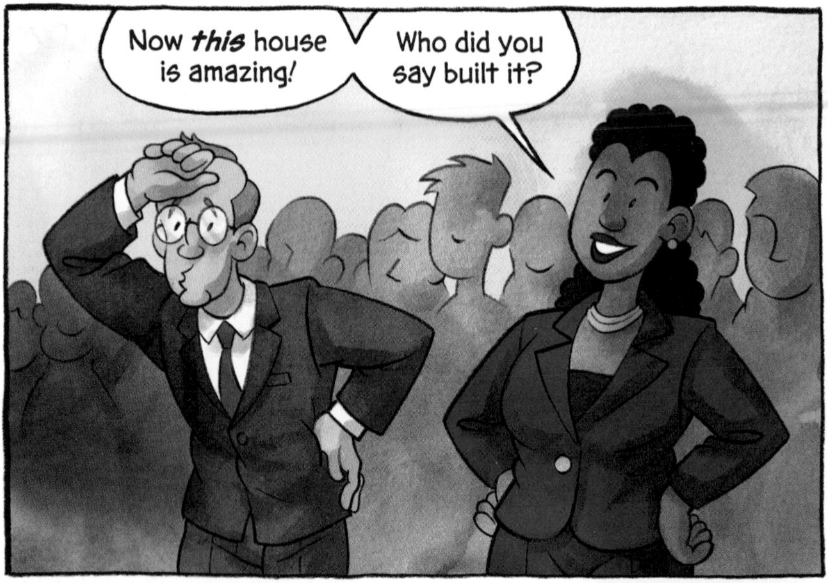
Now *this* house is amazing!
Who did you say built it?

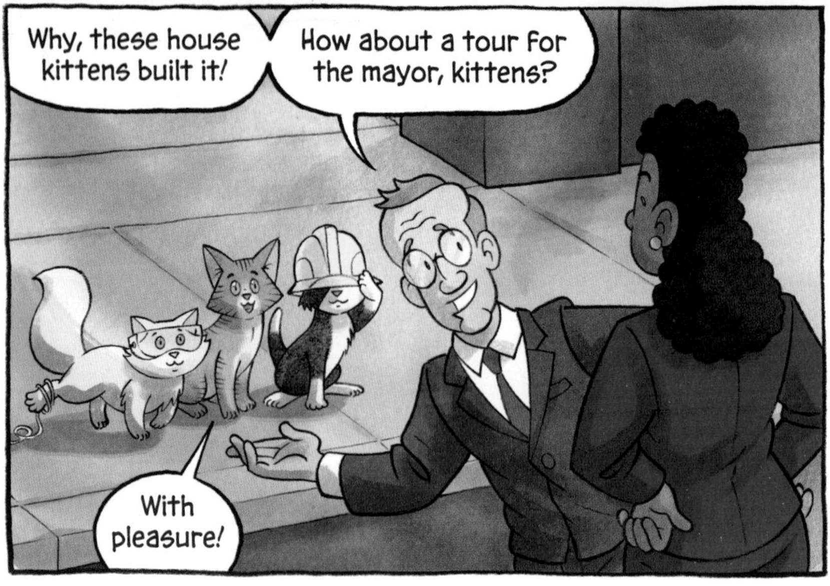
Why, these house kittens built it!
How about a tour for the mayor, kittens?
With pleasure!

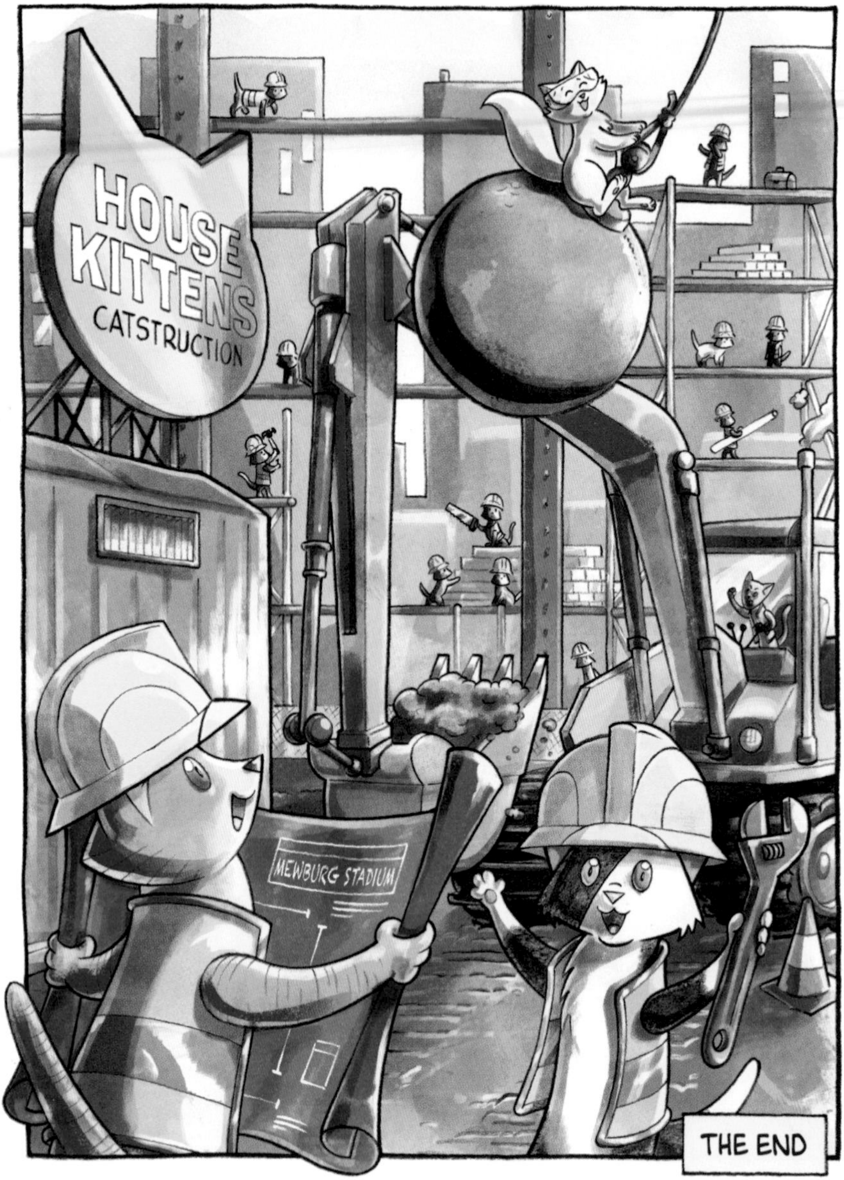
HOUSE KITTENS
CATSTRUCTION
MEWBURG STADIUM
THE END

KITTEN CONSTRUCTION COMPANY

ORIGINAL CHARACTER DESIGNS

The final designs of the House Kittens look a lot like the first versions I drew, with a few minor differences.

Marmalade was originally named Mittens. But since Sampson actually has mittens, it seemed odd that it wasn't his name instead.

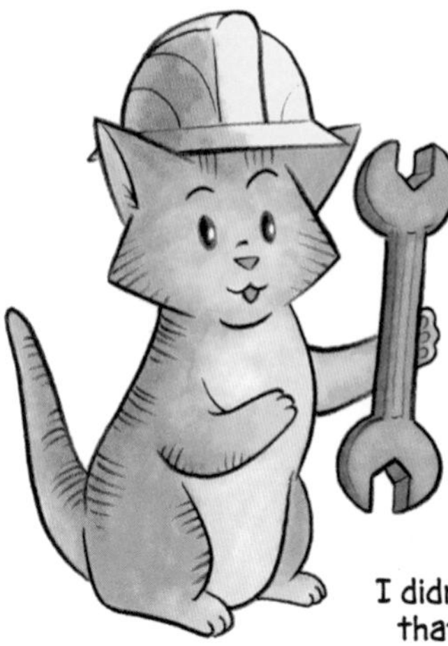

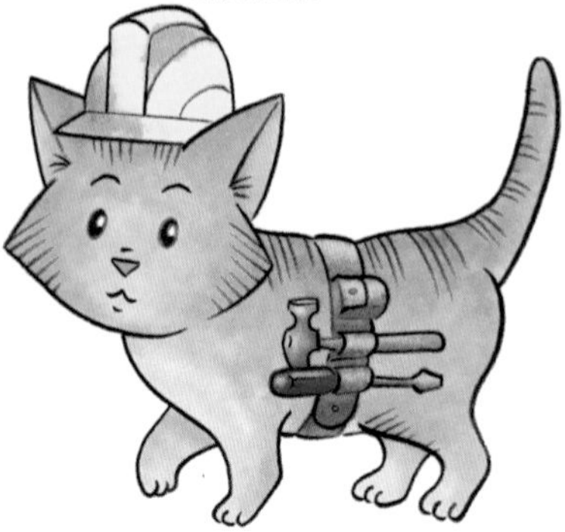

I didn't want two names that started with the letter M, though. The name Sampson seemed like a good fit for his personality.

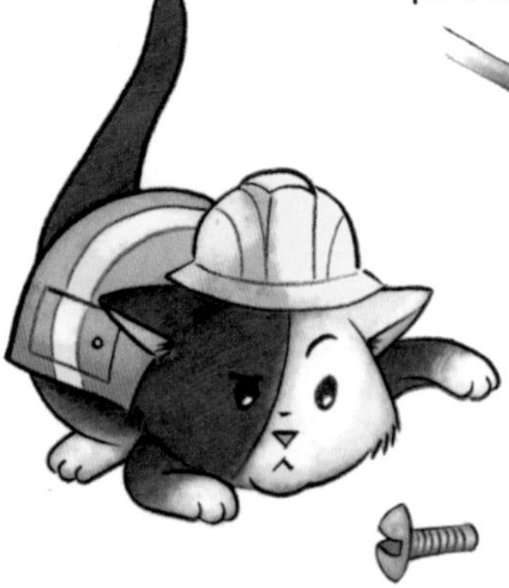

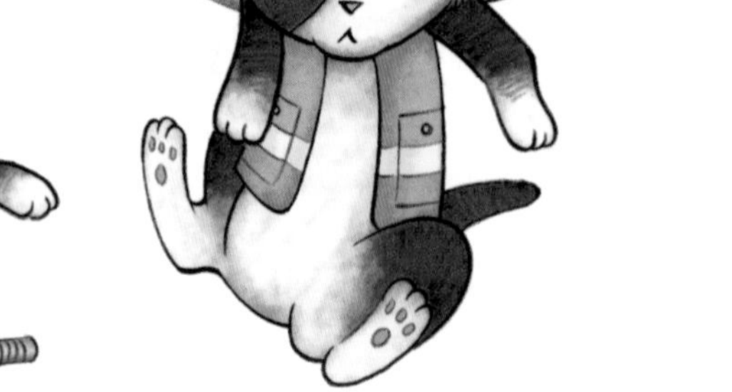

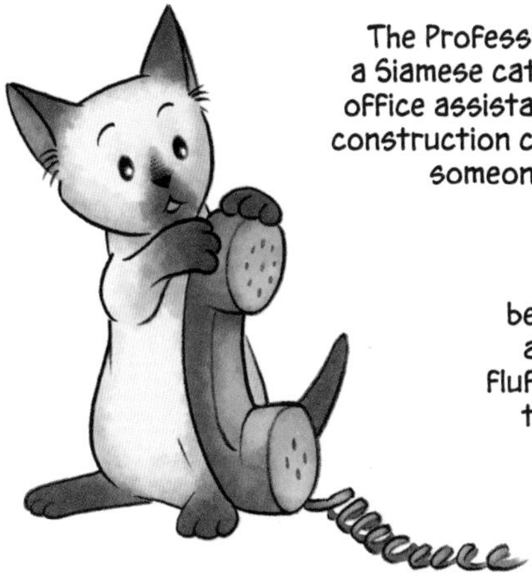

The Professor was always going to be a Siamese cat, but he started out as the office assistant. Maybe when the kittens' construction company expands they'll need someone to man the phones!

Bubbles's name came about because she likes water. She was always a white cat, but her big fluffy tail wasn't added until I drew the first page she appears on!

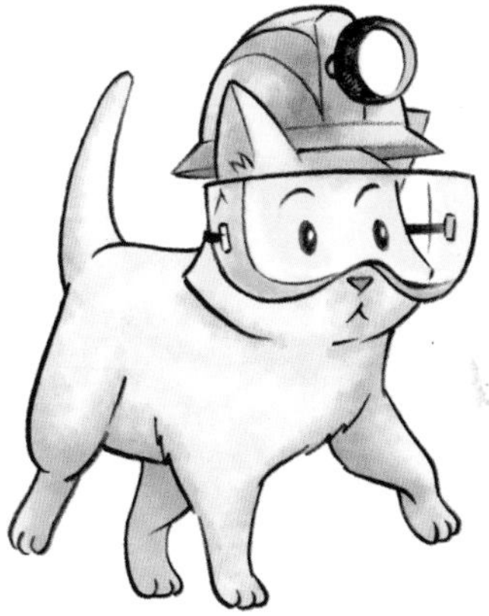

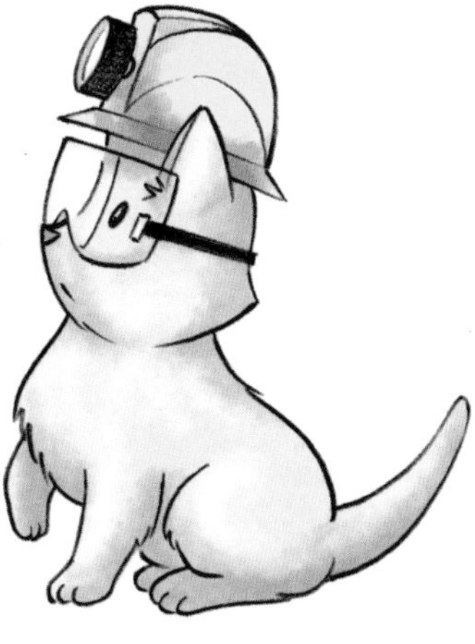

A few cats I designed didn't make it into the story. But maybe you'll see them in the next book!

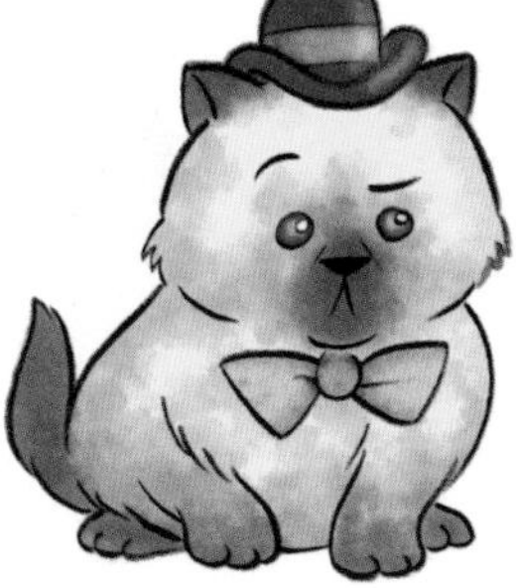

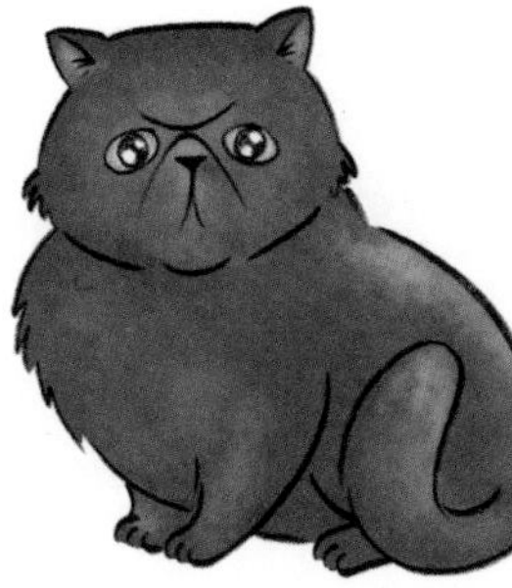

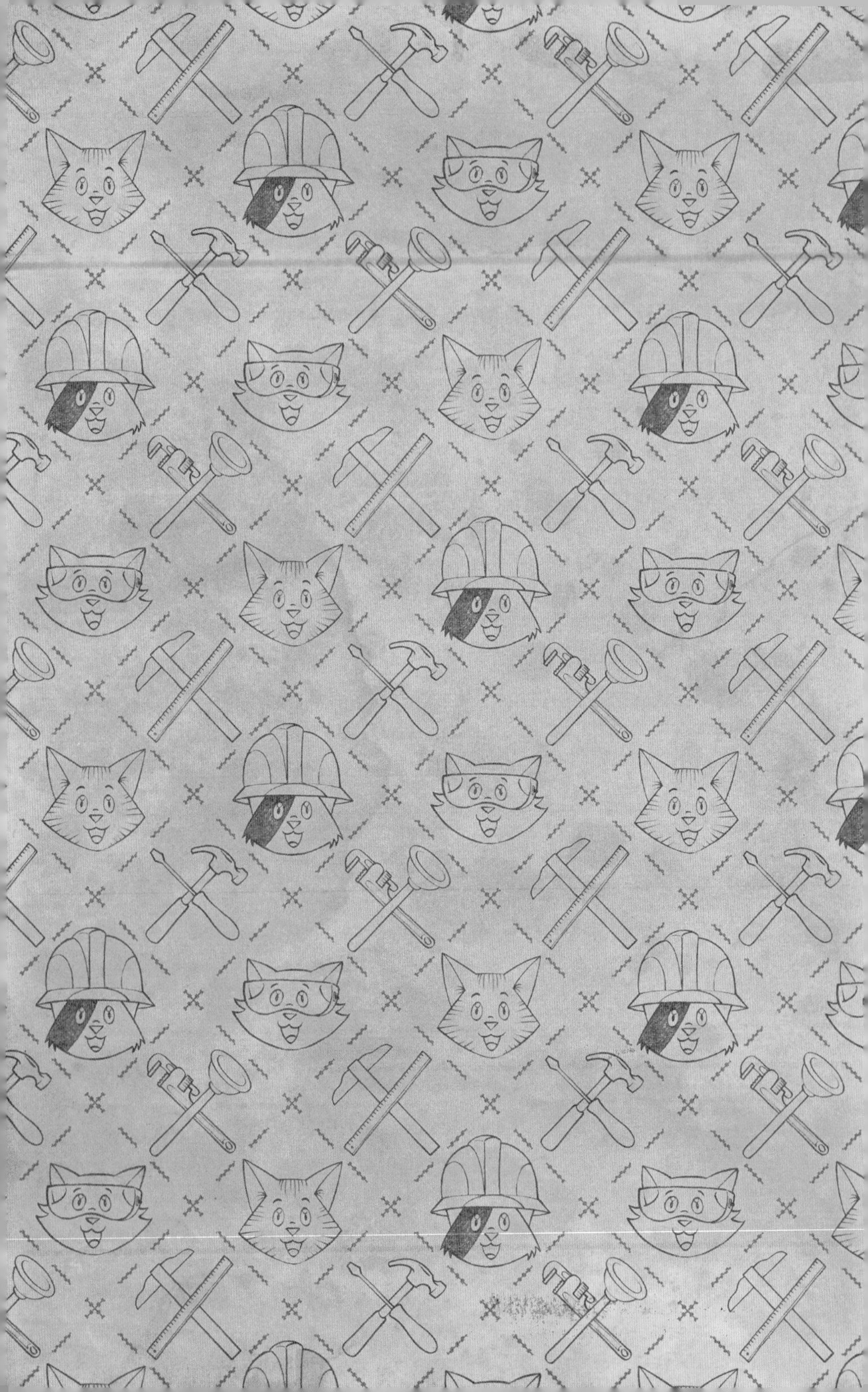